LITTLE DEBBIE CHARIBERT

Don M Denn

Copyright © 2024 DON M DENN

All rights reserved.
No part of this book LITTLE DEBBIE CHARIBERT published by General Publishing, may be reproduced in any form or by any electronic or mechanical means, including information storage and retrieval systems, without permission in writing from the publisher, except by reviewers, who may quote brief passages in a review and certain other noncommercial uses permitted by copyright law.

For permission requests:
Write to the publisher, addressed
"Attention: Permissions Coordinator,"

GENERAL PUBLISHING, Inc

Any references to historical events, real people, or real places are used fictitiously. Names, characters, and places are products of the author's imagination.
Library of Congress Control Number: 1 2 3 4 5 6 7 8 9 10

Printed in The United States of America

Published by: GENERAL PUBLISHING, Inc.
CALIFORNIA

978-2-6248-6097-0

For all good people everywhere

MEET LITTLE DEBBIE

    𝒫ost-haste august Texan tempest, Loving's folks despairingly sentient somewhere close-knit around lone star state –excepting thriving elsewhere sufficed more, witnessed visit town not many weeks yet -minus cousin-flood -descended down upon earth illimitably, scattering many chop-chop away-- others lickety-split hence whence home enchants --but whilst absorbed little Debbie visited Pecos River walk-always delighted accommodating jaywalkers along Loving County's side: seeing countless natural habitats laid waste by awesome forces nature compelled, received serendipitous inspiration modern Loving County must come about utilizing sand mainly, mortar too, molds additionally, 'warrioress' planned transforming every building, nook, cranny Loving boasted - within brown sands beside long stretches solely comprising grasslands, windswept prairies augmenting most areas around, resettling all displaced creatures familiar natural habitats have cradled: once presumed wouldn't provide any botheration; burrows, ant-hills, crevices, holes above-perhaps ones below ground, brush piles, nest boxes, beneath fallen trees, et cetera, creatures-symbolizing statistics beneath one hundred-fifty locals, increasingly derived prominence once important matters tabled.

    Little Debbie detested sitting idle whilst everything laid waste, fixing spiritedly, wanted changes effectuated, Debbie set tasks upon herself encompassing trying local municipality's patience employing ways exceeding any child's authority, none eleven reserved such powers as acting out influences one generation sooner however intelligent, like every other similarly aged child, possessed little knowledge or exact ideas next viable action's situations warranted, sole recurrent thought dictated one action worth taking, meanwhile, Bessie Haynes' ninth grade lessons, alongside countless peers attending Mentone's second elementary schools long situated inside Loving county-listed as not boasting beyond one hundred sixty-eight, Country's smallest county most touted Loving during bygone eras - officially held second rearward position, made certain education progressed smoothly

"Isabella, any superior ideas?" Debbie later questioned one close associates Isabella O'Roehampton habitually - much as Debbie, often thought much prior any responses, on occasion arranged meeting not far off Debbie's inspection spot on waterfront bridges partially victimized through long unattended usage transpired, served good purposes, disrepaired bridges alongside countless other infrastructure clamorously sought attentions alongside countless Mentone's flood damages as well, "given limitless options, I have one: redevelopments,"

"Dearest Debbie, I cannot quite guess utterances required I make, let alone suggest necessities," responded Isabella as soothingly-lounging on young rumps Loving's sandy lakefront busy tossing stones towards Beacon Light lake's direction, continued, Debbie briefly admired Miss O'Roehampton's impeccable logic inherent within keeping lips sealed except proper values accompanied words, "otherwise, I expect no one else expresses my fondness regarding forth coming propositions - irrespectively voiced or not." miss O'Roehampton uttered additionally,

Soon again, firmaments darkened, foreboding inclement weather, perhaps more of precipitation weather persons working TV networks jobs allover deemed rain, not tempest like one observed abate seven hours-no more, little Debbie discerned no reason whatsoever rushing home; perhaps intending staying dry approaching inclemency or not,

"Isabella, let's play lots longer, much time remains, waterfront provides irresistible allure everyone including I as well, honor, one doubts if any more precipitation nears visiting earth anytime soon, though not within one antecedent hour, never mind weather people-"

"Not if I can help matters, Debbie," agreed O'Roehampton, hoping inapparence shielded truths over symbolically maintaining solitude, "but we shouldn't waste any more time," -not certain if Isabella's conclusions enjoyed any concurrence, added–

"We could simmer trepidations-our nearest coteries are quite likely feeling by now over our absences, no how families aren't impatiently awaiting our arrivals-wondering themselves silly everyone knows -oughtn't we rekindle fireplace-togetherness, families deserve good times till insinuated rainfalls reaches earth, say– many hours hence."

Shortly, while lessened rain intensities fell little-little, droplets puncturing low hanging cumulonimbuses dotting Loving's vast blue gray skies, drizzles reached earth augmenting huge floods covering vast earths around, cutting short frolicking girls' adventurous spirits, or dimming each's joyful overwhelms, each really wanted playtimes extended endless hours on end, after all, today weekend-as hearty as ever, breezed past Thursday night, arriving as heartily as countless Fridays previously, seeing entire weeks school work temporarily discontinued till another week school affair naturally resumes control all over again on young Loving County folks pursuing instructions each repeatedly learned often guided each along lives journey.

Another minute, two– heralded initial raindrops, indeed–rain, fell, reinforcing grounds Debbie held onto bidding one cherished friend with whom valued connections transcended duty, adieu - following similar individual resolves inviting earlier departures heading homes situated far apart where opposite town's ends lay inviting irresistibly: not due failed friendships –needs evading inclemency. Most resolutely, rose nitty-grittily-taking compliant heels dashing along Mentone's streets en-route Charibert's bungalow - after bidding farewells. Not far removed whence Debbie destined trek, keen visuals depicted towns-folks assembled outside Chesserbottle's, two homes away, Debbie stopped briefly too, finding out more should satisfy curiosities once aspirations knowing exact transpiration proceeding inside Mr. Chesserbottle's encouraged questioning bystanders. Perhaps somebody died? –or won huge sums state lotteries? Ah! Mrs. Chesserbottle! --perhaps divorce finally terminated long lasting marital partnership leaving Chesserbottle weeping through roofs perpetually shielding heavily pouring precipitation, thereby attracting neighbors?

Very often, ruminations over wisecracks- *'pictures saying thousand words beyond one's spoken*', but lost on words immediately fitting ascribing imageries witnessed as dainty steps conveyed onwards near destination: Chesserbottle's - one or two homes away, closer. Handling issues properly mattered, impelling brief stopovers as now, abeam Hildebald's-teacher Peregrine- often exploited imparting more knowledge outside school hours –Hildebald's situated between two proximate homes; Chesserbottle's on one side, Charibert's on another, provided safe environments one could view goings-on.

Presently, precipitation came down much more intensely but still fell far beneath torrential rainfalls - though perturbed much, Charibert family house resting one home away, or next after second on Pecos's east street, permitted gaining ascertainments, how else could one attain proper wisdoms if elder Chariberts failed messaging stricken Chesserbottles any commiserations. Stopping by, Debbie's determination making discoveries somewhat soared higher within.

Once again, thoughts immersed magically over likely events constituting harebrained locals gathered doing naught much but observe specters neighbor's address provided immediately, given varying circumstances playing– neighborly ordinances dictated everyone present sympathize willfully, maybe empathize, given this unfolding precipitation, observers experienced deeper cravings-- perhaps more profound attempts overcoming disillusionment at stricken neighbor, one isn't certain --otherwise rebound, then head away.

Recently, some reconditioning of mindsets on never condoning bogus perspectives irrespective of topics; people, events, et-cetera, occurred; indeed, one of many beliefs held Loving beautiful beyond measure, even though perceived as one little place, opinions long sprung up based on minute population not due land mass or similar factors –if calculated accordingly; while neighboring counties boasted forty thousands, fifty-thousands easily, yet boasted land mass comparatively less, Loving provided friendliest sky-canopies only one hundred-sixty nine enjoyed endlessly, yet outclassed most counties. Probing thoughts regarding why people wouldn't use heads carried about on shoulders reasonably, proper work thinking's all required sussing any transformations Loving deserved; yes, wondrous utopias, or wonderlands--as supposed, does make up one list existing somewhere Loving ought enlist securely, nothing ever should halt commencements planned anyhow lest viewpoints devolve akin naysayers':- variously well-educated yet resolutely refuses applying better thinking faculties. Little Debbie mentally observed caution over eventual norms thought applied severally through intermittently occurring societal upheavals like neighbors' --why on earth permitting combativeness about herself nor becoming cheeky, being too forward approaching irrelative issues went without real essence.

Appositely accessing instructions inculcated during fostering throughout passing years, Debbie's memories felt refreshed over correlated situations reminiscing Ayleth's diligence -else, every effort could turn out utter failure! -yes blunders, as mother often talked about; intended ensuring Charibert children commanded wonderful outlooks against relentless shortcomings later on during adulthood -not long ago, attempted instilling enterprising thoughts, by enforcing convictions, maybe considerations involving individual outlooks. Little Debbie couldn't yet figure out applicable meanings, but figured apprehensions, correctly guessing matters differed; not exactly- 'one caught between two stools' scenarios, whilst faltering where apprehending situations mattered, also resembled circuitous blessings, otherwise relenting stood stark over usable ideas imbued others over peers often taunted through retaliatory remarks over nonsensical stuff told on some coming events' soaring popularity.

Meanwhile, increased cloudburst somehow propelled cautiously quarrelsome voices from within 24 Pecos nigh, brimming arguments on auditory senses-wished unbattered by offensive noises worsened by sudden twilight hung low over grocery store proprietors' whose front yard's- Loving folks gathered: 24 Pecos Street playing hosts collapsed earlier-on due shoddy building, parts thereof indeed endured dilapidation, encouraging many folks embarking on activities best musterable, efforts required salvaging owner's ego-smeared pride if any remained exploiting soothingly worded agencies. Debbie Charibert thought, *'If all literary fiction written covering Loving county's abode up till lake front ares, are all fractions insightful or enjoyable as current tattletale outside one conversely suggests, most or all'd attain unputdownable classics' status*, folks' presumed fright over general Mentone domiciliarys' conditions an understatement noted contemporaneously common, overwhelms even seasoned someone's setting out on redevelopment quests, but not Debbie Charibert,

"Needless conscience afeard if guilt rests afar," -passed literatures disclosed, perhaps heard somewhere-but elapsed time defies remembrance, pertinent wisdom never mattered more-

Sadly, most Loving vicinities populated by neighborhood-worthy shacks, sorts locals exhibit abashments over when giving narratives - much less dole out invitations, over heart stopping truths concerning conditions, derives as Jurisdictional domiciles as do modern mansions wont on exorbitant valuations accompanied by unforgiving costs often nearing four-fifths less elsewhere, penuriant's should seek out, perhaps-- not New York, not Los Angeles, but; Mentone, or neighbors thereof; Potterville, Hay Flat –even Woody –shades cast by tree branches serving each as saving graces-inhibiting unrelenting elements under unforeseen circumstances obviously approaching, certain willing residents envisaging selves dispossessed, adrift on streets—hobos, wanted avoided come hell or high water. Nightmares equaling previous days' torrential downpours, communicated terrible visions about holding onto one's stead pending in coming killjoys exacting usurpation; thin layers existed between habitable roosts entrusted each by Texan charitable trusts, and continued residential comfort, thus establishes effective dichotomies on housing breakthroughs affecting everyone else similarly situated, otherwise, homes since started positing as hapless decayed sorrowful heaps dotting town's earth's surface, becoming sole pictures council viewed all around, consequently–many nurse constant wishes: -suitably good grasses germinated greener elsewhere, or leastways, hoped council's timely legislation compelled standardizing newfangled instant electromagnetic matter hewer demonstrations elsewhere proved could ensure new edifices hither, ran abreast any thither through quick construction.

Indeed, dwellers; every-one, agreed on self-evident truths savviless authorities have complete awareness many suffered great insecurities surrounding Loving County shacks, taking each close earthquakes shave-as far afield as California provided into account; documentation are abound showing emergency transpirations afterwards, sends every last local straight onto permanent outdoors since cascading shingles isn't one more reality any Mentonian wished assaying, yet haven't responses.

SMILES ONTO OUR PRAIRIES, ONTO OUR

𝓔 vents four days ago passed peacefully, resident neighbors occupying north 24 Pecos Street Mentone - Loving, apparently experienced domestic squabble, or minor misunderstandings-really, not much important one ought spend plenty time pondering thoughtfully - neighbors took accounts during visits whereupon solely assuaged curiosities exceeded twelve, not fifteen people amounting crowds Debbie discussed earlier on. Breaking ground moments arrived Beacon Light, no broods containing nine individuals-as legends normally suggests about rumored 'cause-championing' young females-embellished surroundings using rambunctious personalities perhaps mere presences too, fully knowledgeable as concerns current affairs, waited breathlessly, none else thought caring about well-cemented popularity - as: 'battle on' alone warrioress, mattered -even if whilst searching, also seriously considered relenting, should situation bottom out. Debbie selfishly conserved chosen dates, repeatedly questioning herself how anyone could ever realize such wondrous fancies– not naming anything else we have as viable options? -repeatedly troubled Miss Charibert, as each hunkered down.

Initially, Texan government presented blind senses, every Debbie's serially documented handwritten efforts, engendered laughter around county offices' vicinities, instead showed greater interests attracting lobby alongside oil money or investments–if roused corporations agreed allocating solicitors shares.

Debbie shifted attention; affairs countervailing 'forward children's council' leniently offering membership positions --indeed, as regards Loving, little 'Little Debbie' aged girls served councils, consequently–alongside few friends; Livilda Ravenshield, Elizabeth Hattersley, Zoe Mogridge, not least Camilla Culverwell, also one more, augmented county council's membership lists.

During votes touching county reconstruction, peers ballot ways parents advised: along elders' lines, Debbie's ideas aligned almost against every member's wishes, constantly remained council's young generational nay vote, perhaps due undyingly wanting county reconstruction employing entirely different methods, new County structure, an ultramodern County symbolizing eras ahead, long wanted– reconstructions Loving deserved continued on drawing paper, bedroom floor, through graffiti vacant spaces on walls admitted on one else's behest –Lego city christened Mentone, as wide spread information promised everyone somewhere around lay one unspecified dream place verily understood equaled Utopia, Hewntopia, or Wonderland by Beacon light forever willfully issuing each person within locality -again all theoretically, visitation rights whereupon planned construction site should reveal modern marvels, afterwards give feedbacks.

Adventurous little Debbie Charibert incontrovertibly enjoyed familiarities beyond immediate Mentone locality –attributes every parent numbering not beyond thirty or forty anyhow, but nonetheless remained Loving's parents still, strict through PTA injunctions, voted upholding school children's welfare, or wishing school received better care. Children gutsy attributes endured - as noticed lately, one habit parents hoped quickly-as permanently pushed necessary inculcation children required approaching adulthood-forward, hopefully, those kids look back pridefully –remembering parents laying good foundations offspring's still ongoing onward journey relies on, Debbie however trusted taking matters steps further, energetic, perhaps feisty, even venturesome, several close associates previously suggested overconfidence was an urgent issue, on each occasion, sought after sources such attributes originated, since detecting equivalent's whatsoever within elder Charibert lady, proved impossible -Buchard Charibert never betrayed remote signs either.

Little Debbie often identified such people as irrelevant moronic fools utterly wanting true knowledge, one could simply find attributively enhanced individual behaviors without forcible inculcation by parents–not least peer pressure, fools others fancy ought flaunt ease of living, or acknowledge great fortunes someone such as none other, partied alongside, taking friends forward.

Yes, accepting designation suggesting 'adventurousness', 'determined', 'undaunted', even belligerent–assuming matters subsumed opinions whether propounded ideas reached adoptable or acceptable standards, forever resolutely declining any dissuasions by cynical others whilst pursuing pressing matters –regarding upcoming proposed Mentone's brittle sand built New Loving's Lego city –loose sands everyone veritably understands, never quite augured well pertaining buildings' structural durability, but anyways, Mentone's beach low sand dunes originating New Loving neared, employing bare knuckles alone till New Lego city structure stood tall, little Debbie promised much blasts assigning Charibert name historical values, crying over spilt milk maden't much sense, Loving County-incorporated twice, first during 1800's epoch, county's founder: one mister -guess who? -Oliver Loving –consequent upon sustaining injuries local Indians meted, chose acting courageously; following legendary stories, proceeded, shortly afterward, Loving County posed its initial Phoenix rising, though never rose, till this day no one knows why county population steadfastly maintains minimal counts well below two hundred, once numbers reduced beneath twenty during historic periods preceding eras minerals discoveries brought enterprising families already hunkered down elsewhere – back with all those preconceived notions now needing eventuating oppositely.

Besides upcoming estates occupying entire thought processes, little girl's 'big mindedness': title proudly toted about lately whilst spotted wielding big sticks, little Debbie Charibert–twice during past few days, went about drawing patterns depicting New Loving maps on Beacon Light lakefront; building blocks occupied one place, incongruous drawings depicted roundabouts as circles, lines drawn indicated highways showed somewhere else, somewhere proximate- inscribed mountains, hills, lakes, rivers, several divergent features good topographies boasted --fought over places on one sandy patch bordering Beacon Light, many more indistinct features followed dexterous fingers traveling zig-zagedly over beige sand. Today of all days became Debbie's own long awaited 'breaking ground day'. Little Debbie smiled broadly as good process continued, none else could see this developing vision, all required go-n't past standing erect, still, envisaging sprawling 'Loving' standing majestic right within visual acuities, slender arms waving past dreamy eyes sometimes caused New Loving's temporary vanishing, upon shutting two blue eyes once again, visualizes upcoming majestic edifices few feet away: New Loving, stand tall, most really, another Phoenix rising Texas bound –pertinently, New Phoenix rising ought rear upwards through ornamenting sand grains– watch out-all! –folks'll see how many possessed dexterities rendered such daunting matters facile, devolved onliest topics resigned reckoning created within endless unprompted internal dialogues–

"Phoenix rising,"

"Phoenix rising? -Explain please, Phoenix rising?"

"I suppose –fabled instances where whimsical houses grew up suddenly, till people leased or rented domiciles,"

"Yes, I believe I do,"

"Remember? –mother divulged whiles back 'phoenix rising', I remember strange appellations during conversation, we'd soon have one gracing Mentone,"

"Oh yes, yes, I remember,"

Vocally accentuating beliefs constructing majestic cities as New Loving promises, needn't take much efforts, little Debbie struck poses crossing both arms over yet unmatured chest parts, thereafter, invoked yet again great visions encompassing 'Wonderland Loving', or Utopian County, or whatever some envisaged somewhere brimming tall towers befitting New York city's–one needed strapping themselves atop earth's surface as preventive efforts, gazing up caused many tippings over, one held on till one falls down whilst beholding wondrous marvels. Undaunted, Debbie bumptiously attached already over laden blueprints additional features, efforts required peeling certain lineaments away regardless whether whatever part Debbie initially added forms required augmentation, enhancing adjoining Loving's constituents consequential on each interconnected functionalities inside proposed Loving. Vacation endured, Debbie's position convinced everyone no one's diligences could possibly disavow going forward building New Loving whether deep within dreams or not, if present County executives: certain relatives inclusive, unrelated others similarly, continued shying away once queries required responses vis-à requests allocating construction permits covering any ultramodern town or cities -New Loving County inclusive, thereafter bequeath all good county folks inhabitable spaces alongside every Charibert.

SCREAMS AT THE WIND:

  *L*ittle Debbie Charibert's construction gradually neared commencement, each morning during this holiday season, neighbors notice recurrent Beacon Light visitation - bearing purposive odds additionally augmenting practical bits brought along - minding each one's usefulness, hoping said odds, or ends, helped pepped up blueprint's features, additionally, somehow imbue prominent features greater value.

  County executives-certain each one's capabilities measured insignificantly shorter than Debbie's heroics, too- refused relenting, though not as assertive as Mentone's little upcoming compatriot, none about possessed any muster let alone-boldness challenging visiting broad brimmed hatted Texas executives detailed around recently-inspecting everywhere, eagerly chasing down any errors whatsoever, one flimsy fault seemed all melancholiacs required in disqualifying entire Loving County projects disregarding Debbie's constant negative vote if propositions supported someone else's ideas; all proffered ideas till date somehow disappointed standards ultramodern cities must resemble inside out, or-- ones favored during council balloting.

  Holiday season neared rather too quickly, bringing-Christmas weeks away, nigh'r. Notwithstanding Debbie's great ambitions, events completely forecasted impossibilities around Loving's advent prior several Santa Claus'es driving reindeer sleighs, transporting holiday gifts young locals craved--into town, wanted on any real feasibility especially self-conservation since children's attention suddenly reckoned Saint Nick, hence cleverly avoided unnecessary hurry; more Christmases lay ahead; one right after one approaching, one right afterwards, another thereafter, but presently, hunkering down on 'project Loving' -an onliest existing, or kicking off constructions smoothly, listed as premiere priorities.

  Four days later, morning's particularly breezy weather failed deterring little Debbie forthcoming Beacon Light bound estates still –unbeknownst everyone-including peers attending elementary school Debbie studies—otherwise would duly inform Debbie beforehand, several workmen cladding hard hats colored; red, yellow, others white, awaited, two staged rude interruptions, hollering vociferously, perhaps-shouting often solved constructions worker's problems, apparently, much hopes rested on intimidating behaviors passing across urgent points,

"Kid, leave! -out!-out!!" -one's increased decibels suggested suppressed anger,

"No business ought bring little ones here, road graders are about–" -another's demand further accentuated first fellows unequivocal positions, "hear me? -we say– remove yourselves abruptly!""Don't take such embittering tones on us, little girls detest such –we'll cry foul!" threatened Debbie just as one unnamed peer began whimpering,

"But we won't," promised Livilda additionally moments prior blue hat clad outwardly incensed construction hard hat's formulated reply, "mean grownups needn't go around mistreating little girls however pleasurable," Livilda's additional remarks, particularly set worsening situation up,

"Get out kid! -caterpillar approaches!" Hard hatted men's angry voices continued reaching waterfront warrioresses,

"But we won't, we presume your persons are suspects about doing county some really bad deal," continued Debbie borrowing one leaf Ayleth's defiant words discharged conversationally numerous times while shopping groceries each time store keepers hoped finessing more bean product's profits during transactions, "perhaps we can solicit your peaceful but hasty departure --certain ideas represent my plot-readying germinating new Mentone, new Loving, new country," "But we insist, or we'll attempt changing your attitudes some other way," promised Eardwulf Thornwood -Booth's associates, moments antecedent boss's interruption stilled working crew's subordinate voice following realizations analysis attributed warrioresses efforts may contain small indecipherable errors,

"Please, please do consider our company persuaded," -Booth's concession indicated fear or reluctance fighting young girls, tackling matters involving minors never suited anyone, not least gruff unkempt construction workers holding firm underneath morning's gray skies, however, immediate desistance opposing girls construed diversely depending on each person's perception apropos lowered brash tones spoke volumes -at any rate, threats registered, despite four young female's tough showing, employment related tasks nested all around workmen must accomplish, apparently, men cladding wrought on egocentric conceit following rough manners entered Loving's redevelopment picture,

"Yeah, right!" Thornwood scoffed somewhat indifferently, another county contractor rather sheepishly, avoiding further offending morning's rivals - lest any further continuance Booth wished-covertly bringing company's earth moving equipment alive worsen situation, perhaps kicking off humankind's all time's greatest contest on Mentone's Gettysburg battlefield-Debbie comparatively interpreted current daily situations –though soon, clever lever manipulations disclosed erroneous presumptions Lake front girls bandied about over caterpillars driver immediate intentions, for-moments later reversed backwards-billowing plentiful thick sooth almost two or four yards beneath intertwining roundish low hanging cloud plumes hovering above, easily constituting environmental pollution likes-over which someone someplace suffered incapacitation within minutes, another somewhere dead inside one hour-no more.

Onward–arguments endlessly continued, sometimes friendly, on occasions-heated, but Debbie's apprehensions strengthened even as five working men vented rages, trepidations prevented further approaches on areas Debbie stood inspecting visual renditions upcoming New Loving estate presented oneirically, each workman dreaded potential county charges of harassing nine or eleven year olds somewhere about town; elementary school ages sufficed girl's understanding - several laws prohibited grown men addressing unrelated elementary age ones, such realizations revived mental fortification enabling staying put, refusing any movements even as continuing vociferousness-but also finger-pointing worsened, those foolhardy men dared scream themselves hoarse, after all, girl's attitude failed omitting daringness, or likely, merely another young local seriously revising county history repeatedly, besides setting up corrective maneuvers for grwn people's attitudes.

Minutes preceding simultaneous strong worded rebuke three workmen handed much younger female locals - working girls mentally improvised battling if Debbie must prevail without stepping aside - due this, preventing earth moving bulldozer's pass, warrioress trio; Livilda, Zoe accompanied by Camilla, three closest friends, suddenly appeared, each one's presence gracing Debbie's stance. Envisaging hardships once pondering's projected afore-anticipated difficulties working manual labor alone involved, soliciting by invite's ways, reached schoolmates through rapid scamperings by another- but unsung peer: Mirabel Conrad chanced by on family errand, recognized—not just Debbie alongside Livilda, but impending situation as well, abandoned errand once embarking en-route Mentone town square with news promising good work assisting New Loving redevelopment registered

Many pleas swayed hearts, attentive ones toting two helping hands each, agreed coming over upon deliberations prior paying each sometime later, subsumed many heartfelt thanks, supporting good causes comprised morals everyone's parents always counseled about: repaying kind deeds once earliest opportunities come calling, associates congregated alongside Mirabel Conrad, later concurred with Debbie's supplications.

Meanwhile, working girls looked, observing one laborer: one wearing red hard hat, perceived by all four enterprising girls as one psychologist naturally think wouldn't let sleeping dogs lie, rev Caterpillar's earth mover's engines, although, running children over however, never constituted Booth's immediate considerations.

All enthusiastic presumptions by men folk - many years advanced beyond fathers rearing these eleven-year-olds, proved right, momentarily, or two seconds later, battled scurrying away frightened: workmen's anticipated response, no less one hoped issued alongside loud revs, Caterpillar bulldozer reversed, slowly beforehand, but incrementally as tracks removed operations farther away letting Debbie's crew three- or plus one-half yards breathing spaces McKenzie's & Co's earth moving equipment could not startle.

Loving girls hadn't defied McKenzie operational machinery's anyhow, previous dusk fell whilst Caterpillar held positions exactly on spots Sunday night descended-halting activities--including Caterpillars often annoying growls -two or three odd yards away behind blueprint's western--most parts duly dubbed 'Lego city on Beacon Light' even if built entirely using good Loving beach sand, apparently, prohibitive fears gripped morning's adversaries hence bulldozer's procrastination running over Debbie's Loving. Eardwulf Thornwood, Caterpillar driver priming work activities, readily boarded caterpillar's cabin thinking revving up engines better prepared, even saved young adversaries little Debbie Charibert's resolute self-assertive venturesome crew stood gathered hoping defiance ultimately enabled successful bare knuckles installation of Debbie's ultramodern County, mishaps morning's major aggressor intended.

"Yayy!" screeched Zoe, Camilla stood by relishing initial victories, facial sneers - often rationale instigating contention between two rivalrous peers herself, Livilda - on past issues, but today, gained as one formidable instrument furthering derision,

"Hee--haw!" exclaimed Livilda--sounding enchantingly Texan, hands thrown upward exhilarated.

"Now we're talking!" declared one: Landgrave Dickens, aloud–whilst making more condescending utterances meanwhile-

"Alright, have your way, we'll see how far much courage goes, silly girls!"

"We'll see!" Debbie's incensed agreement reached right back–as Booth's caterpillar operatives-it suddenly appeared-intended inviting appropriate county authorities-detailing eager arresting constables, but, should matters devolve so– ten visions would behold one young female steadfastly making herself one reluctant companion worth observing–

Under certain circumstances namely; courtesy, politeness obliging past occasions, Debbie's attitude permitted leniency, but– today's grownups just faltered immaturely – as once again, engines revved, tracks moved forward briefly.

Other caterpillar working crew stood gazing, hands tied over Debbie's daring defiance, but– another one: Livilda, emerged hysterical, forcing working men's or adversaries' immediate considerations as too feisty, too irredeemably resolved on standoff. Soon after hysteric screaming began-upon internal hexagonic imageries projecting McKenzie's Caterpillar bulldozer running attending friends over, registered on hers alongside three more feeble minds, attending peers acted appropriately. Feeling somewhat irrelevant, Zoe joined by Camilla had also enlisted efforts crying; suspicion Caterpillar's wheels approached doing one great irreversible impairment on Debbie, evidently overwhelmed. Debbie's assistive trio however stopped abruptly on seeing Eardwulf Thornwood's heavy equipment halt at once before covering respectable distances reversing away rather than making further forward movements closing gaps. All seven caterpillar men held positions five yards behind bulldozer's final reversal point - glad chosen stance omitted any errors - as yet. Time wore on as few rested wearied selves awaiting County executives terminating events on arrival as agreed upon during preceding telephone conversations few minutes ago summoning help against complaints hereof several imperious defiant girls availing smallish physiques as impediments against construction progress.

Unrelenting rumors anent people refusing Loving's redevelopment any endorsements spread lately, most felt consternation about activities summing constituting: 'highly dangerous ill-conceived childish endeavor, many more suspected brains-behind harbored deep within diverse viewpoints phenomenally bogus, nonetheless, currently ensuing morning's incident convinced Mr. Thornwood's loyal team, five local girl's position: squaring up against McKenzie's bulldozer, equaled hearing Loving county's 'horse's mouth' speak, Thornwood's boys needed no extra convincing, many since determining local folks –not least, scored as far afield as Texas, armed themselves against unwelcome change visiting town, excepting if forecasted changes inarguably resulted– or is executed by local homegrown experts, profit margins weighing considerably, but Miss Charibert partly detested, hence circuitous beratement hard working men earned themselves,

"I couldn't imagine any worse improper actions by grown up anywhere–"

"We have plenty work," Livilda agreed, not exactly certain understandings hoped grasped hearing sassy back talk, succeeding comments- *'we have plenty work',* however proved sufficient.

Morning's victory over idiotical half-witted nuts- harassing ambitious girls required celebrating, all gladly rejoiced seeing 'whose rear sides' ran away, four little girls; Debbie Charibert accompanied by friends Livilda, Zoe, Camilla-moreover, stylishly uncorked four soda pops loudly, soon after quenched party's collective thirsts desiring more victories.

Seven construction workers joined by another twelve awaiting work commencements formed defiant stances opposite four over-ambitious girls auspiciously doubtful blueprint patterns delineated on lake Loving's shore grounds represented much, pursuing subtle manners, matters involving four younger county folks passed off without further incident as opposed diving headlong challengingly, or forcefully removing determined young ladies; one -- Emmett Booth's, Eardwulf Thornwood's Caterpillar driving staff secretly wished daughter Janet Booth personated sometime.

VOIDED WHISPERS

Soon enough, sundry locals learned little Debbie Charibert's warrioresses's braced themselves onto stringent attempts bettering daily affairs - scanty residents inhabiting Loving County managed. Among others aware circulating tales however tall however minuscule, contained amidst constituents; land grabbers embarkation on campaigns–threatening none particularly, but threatening anyhow. Though widely recognized as fact - usurpers often flexed muscles-threatening anyone covertly assisting attempts exerted by 'those faceless little warrioresses', as unrelenting fables designated, locals immediately presumed authorities officially permitted greater inroads Mentone's continuing private activities truly deserved, by granting land development embarkation licenses, being as how two-no more - county folks showed unflinching interests on matters near which others compellingly flaunted utter indifference, disinterest wasn't disturbance anyone fretted about, otherwise, group adapted outlooks accommodating every achievable effort within personal arsenals by accepting counsel on whatever efforts young Debbie Charibert insisted embarking on seeing travails through.

Thursday evening, Debbie's father reestablished patriarchal presence once county offices work terminated, belatedly announcing how spreading information stated certain quirky little girl, or girls - Mentone called daughters, hoped doing redevelopment wonders, rebuilding-perhaps resituating Loving County somewhere uncertified news suggested characterized continuing attempts bettering everyone's lots. Debbie sat easily, eavesdropping as senior Chariberts' conversation knowingly centered topics on Beacon Light exploits during morning's discussions, propositions precluded befuddling anyone - much like corrupt County executives, inclusive or exclusive-depending on particular information one possesses –respecting those unrelated or familiar ones amongst state executives-perhaps county officials detailed over, always endorsed through active involvements people observed continued: pulling wool over people's eyes making empty redevelopment pledges none ever sees bear fruits hence after over one hundred fifty years, Loving hardly took steps beyond remaining small-boasting under two hundred people distributed all over its expanse, though per capita income enjoyed by select resident families here-like O'Roehampton's: chocolate chip factory owner, Van Lindens: Oil magnate, surprisingly maintained higher ranking - as best America boasted; let no one take any already earned Loving accolades away, county folks-reputedly indifferent on such disturbing questions, once again agreed, leaving matters thereat whenever arguments reached thence, but still--

Debbie's eavesdropping continued, enabling younger immature ear's grasping entire contents thereof as Mister Charibert's insinuations bearing upon overwhelming curiosities killing cats, as one expects regarding immediate situation, suggestions entailed those little kids: meaning:- Debbie Charibert: daughter --though unaware much personal adjacencies carried Charibert's household alongside on going Lakefront development puzzle, warrioresses too, were bound on identification one day soon, thereafter shed more light on situations.

Responses followed forthwith, Ayleth Charibert accessing usual summative reflections, suggested matters naturally rested squarely on Loving county's government: meaning relatives-additionally - but also those unfamiliar others inhabiting Texas --persistent mantras included attempting beguiling redevelopers-howsoever-- into worthy activities, further opining all- those little girls remarks mentioned, petitioned Loving County's ennoblement - placing nation's most humble abodes on par counties' all over.

But Buchard Mr. Charibert wouldn't have foolish suppositions, imprudence surrounding managing matter by small children steadily worsened bewilderment -- for encompassing situations people clearly noted-suggested everyone thrived off shaky rockers in remotely entertaining abandoning redevelopment if implicit within circulating stories, county offices condones along official ranks, powerful officials choosing adjusting protocols allowing kid's exploits - bandied about as dauntless, contained truths,

"Really, situations aren't far cries simulating reasons Loving County stalled always till date, oughtn't authorities simply incarcerate those kids?"

"Oh my! --every bit some silly talk have I heard uttered all day dear? -imprison children? --thereafter indifferently maintain unconcerned outlooks on unfortunate children's well beings?" Too tired hearing illogical argument Mr. Charibert retired, bedtime beckoned too greatly, futilities dogging tonight's rest tormented Buchard's urgent needs, rest topping priorities --though planned thinking more whilst unwinding. Truly, no one managed attaining ascribable interpretations warranting assigning, also, nobody deciphered any credible reasons making such suggestions over little girls' actions, by which doing, avoid taking authorities too seriously. Stopping briefly beside Debbie doing homework, conducted brief scrutinies-sitting a minute or two, moments thereafter, affectionately patted young one's shoulder,

"Good child, Debbie, wonderful Christmas gifts awaits your receipt soon," hollered Mr. Charibert--bungalow's main bedroom doing little good enabling Ayleth's hearing, in all probabilities, Mr. Charibert hoped Debbie--seated across expansive 23 Pecos street's dining room heard, "keep up efforts, I'm sure any anticipated good'll follow your endeavors doing homework as has my Little Debbie all evening, situation'll pan out well within fullness of time,"

"Thanks father," replied Debbie shifting away tired eyes since layered over spread schoolbook pages poured halfway through, as viable conversation's worthy words formulated more replies-- "I'm certain your understandings include - affairs aren't merely about speed racing, or finish lines, Christmas season approaches, everyone spends time catching up on life's affairs, especially extracurricular activities plus fun-family deserve partaking, I should not show displeasures if frolicking about outdoors prove too overwhelming. Take time off, visit friends, visit Beacon Light, note your most valuable personal skills, make wonderful memories outdoors, bring back great ideas Loving's horizons could be broadened by, think my advice over, dear, alright?" -apparently, Mr. Charibert secretly wished daughter maintained any complicity whatsoever with those little girls triggering much circulating rumors.

"Certainly," replied Debbie Charibert uncertainty over interpretations Buchard Charibert's remarks deserved, not quite an hour, held unwavering position implying impermissibility, unflinchingly awaiting certain young towns native's activities; young girls, especially one currently bent over homework alongside dear father, comprehended herself as being --even suggesting throwing each person involved far into incarceration sounded right –but suddenly, here Buchard Charibert stood, offering Beacon Light personal visitation whereupon make memories -memories? Whatsoever could ever make one better memories above building new headquarters Loving thereafter calls Loving County? –going ahead somewhere around Loving's waterfront authorities christened Beacon Light long ago?

Exercising patience till Buchard Charibert dozed off short moments later, approached Ayleth apparently realizing some education on exact meanings hoped conveyed by those utterances, was proper. Debbie desired explanation why chosen positions deviated sitting undecidedly atop high fences on current matter, as one expected whenever hopping all over running county errands, hassling authorities-sometimes entertaining warlike demeanors whilst treating pressing matters requiring immediate resolution; redevelopment projects, road mending, weren't unreasonable requests -whilst inebriated.

VULTURES AND BANDITS

Several days later, young Debbie realized how much previous day's waterfront standoff against duly employed workmen harnessing great heavy bulldozer, all observed work variously --upon recognizing one additional gambit: 'vultures' Debbie preferred as suitable appellatives men variously referenced as bandits by various diverse groups-deserved, vultures being politicians perpetually awaiting every given opportunity aforementioned 'vultures' intended making good on individual political careers, bandits being corporations, corporate executives, or sinister county agents manipulating government systems previously successful goons through which each accrued quick fossil fuels finances employing very corrupt means.

Unsubdued, as Debbie– always accompanying three little friends love presuming gains on understandings over how much impudence surrounded facing off against powerful circles considering unchecked little quests building new counties, perhaps appropriating whatever resources attainable by yet feeble hands, without much endorsement given by well positioned folks; wherefore being stalwarts, if-n't doomed? -or, if not failure outright, one's never successful undertaking any venture,

"Interesting events everyone says-" Debbie explained hoping inherent meanings delightfully satisfied Livilda's comprehension; boredom however motivated several morning's hence:– though now two or three days ago's-visitation, whereat congratulated themselves on staging one unexpected victory over caterpillar working men. Joyous memories regurgitated freshly each passing day within warrioresses' minds, till another standoff reared days later—staging encore performances, though-only reversing imposing bulldozer ten or twenty yards away, comprised totally noticeable action Booth's men undertook today, county workmen stood little ways off observing four unmannerly Loving County girls yet again during plucky moments opposing likely situations similarly aged-utterly afeared girls felt anxious about -but given warrioresses' recalcitrant natures, heedlessly obstructed earth moving equipment once more.

Three days ago correlated events transpired, here today: Little Debbie's currently 'on-going' return visits Ravenshields household long expected, homely location Debbie acknowledged happily hosting Ravenshields women; Albree-alongside daughter Livilda, still discussing current events chief'd by circulating lakefront exploits, as tales out-heighting each reached towns person's understandings. Much as learned later, Livilda-too wanted on courage-faltering on intimating folks about explosive questions hinting involving peculiar young culprits executing rumored projects. Debbie's guess topics dominating talking points long seconds after arrival as not overtly important or anything else - Livilda executed habitual finger over lip signal, immediately throwing Debbie some caution, moods each hoped rendered revealing difficult secrets surrounding lakefront standoff, remained prevalent.

Once Albree closed out on quibbling endlessly over foolish overambitious little girls squaring up against dangerous uncaring bulldozer workmen somewhere: new twists stories circulating grapevines bore, Ravenshield household's living room adjusted accordingly, accommodating further gossiping ladies centering on topics rife all over,

"Hey, greetings?" began Debbie tentatively once Mrs. Ravenshield left earshot, "I am hoping our courage," –insinuated courage circuitously hinted flattery or-- if Livilda's own dwindling courage, "isn't going south already?"

"Debbie?" -challenged Livilda, "uttering such indicates deviance on our parts, after all, we're about kick starting great waves,"

"All right!" decided little Debbie-tagging along Livilda's thought patterns, by issuing dearest subtle reminders- good reason abounded firmly-harnessing proper arguments favoring decent directives imbibed during past conversations, Livilda temporarily struck as– to all including Debbie, one given or circuitously seized operational mantles, poising leading warrioress' little fanfare, as well as all observable situations, Debbie owned all resulting spectacles, uniquely reserving authority efforts warranted apropos properly directing Loving redevelopment matters, thence ensured exact information reached Livilda, hopefully soften personal approaches next time chance encounter around adults, or county officials, or waterfront construction workmen, occurred lest adult presume young miss Ravenshield—charge over drive.

Exploiting advantageous situations, Livilda posed demands wanting knowledge-why Debbie paid Mentone's waterfront unscheduled visits during early morning hours, as indicated by wristwatch dials-quoting she - as not yet 8 AM days ago, admitting intrinsic explanations propositions entailed –admittedly, facts evaded closest friends' grasp still, each continued wallowing, oblivious over erecting New Loving County populated by arguably Texas' most decent people - dwelling tall skyscrapers, ones New York City skyscrapers envied.

Morning four days ago saw Livilda Ravenshield, Zoe Mogridge alongside Camilla Culverwell representing agreed phone summons rendezvousing friends found events pleasurable –during specific times, discussed matters earnestly,

"Plans have reached final points commencing blueprints development suiting my New Loving development –Loving County, entering upon beginnings waterfront deserved –but we encountered silly Bulldozers men wearing intimidating hard hats too,"

"Oh, I see," –now, each apprehended peer's visions encompassing oncoming good Mentone ought anticipate,

"Propositions does not necessarily highlight any confidence on my part Livy, nor hint on allowable concessions, concerned individuals hoping someone mounted sufficient aggressions stand better chances halting unwarranted development, ones quite obviously not properly befitting Mentone folk's anyhow,"

"Seriously– how else could anyone possibly mean aggression?"

Both girls' almost voiceless conversations continued inside Ravenshield household's dimly lit living room spotting onliest blue light sources reaching them through one adjacent window, thick blinds - like blinded all windows thereabout, pushed aside partially, admitting light,

"We hadn't exhibited any aggressions Livy; nor started fights, I reposed privately passing time drawing blueprints, instances antecedent unto more McKenzie's Caterpillar bulldozer roars caused disruptions, frightfully I should add, prompting immediate summons warrioresses acknowledged, good fortune your trio arrived soonest, heavens knows subsequent becomings thereafter-hadn't three great friends appeared quickly, bad people hide little children's remains underneath unmoved earth –moreover, mother calls taking unflinching stand: civil rights! –maintaining one's own position–oh! -well, until caterpillars run children over, thereafter, matters alter–"

Anxious over satisfactorily responding Debbie Charibert answers over missing children hiding underneath sand dunes, Livilda Ravenshield taunted,

"Debbie, our next activities entails? –suggestions please–"

"Hold your horses-I say," Debbie appreciated Livilda relinquishing controls – in asking activities entailing what next, "-cross all our fingers, by evening, resolutionary mojo's we could employ on kick-starting new Loving'll present themselves, never mind ill-informed grownups, my schemes aren't dumb, or childish, do bet your bottom dollar-"

SYMBOLIC SPECTACLE

*A*pparently, little Debbie Charibert's resolve about making Loving County - parts unknown hoped inhabiting, reflected through every activity tackled, indicatively, eagerly awaited undertaking meaningful chores ad-libitum. Debbie–too wise an eleven year old, never **been** one– although still too young –reprehensibly irrational every occasion embarkation on quests resulted, harnessing entirely unwavering reputation seeing whatever endeavors embarked on till final moments tasks ends; all inhabiting Loving County: all one hundred ninety six people; friends, relatives-plus all consenting-little Debbie, or if another– whomever fit descriptions, appeared too far along resituating Loving anew, notwithstanding, myriads awaited prayerfully, hoped little Debbie Charibert succeeded on everyone's behalf; every last one's hometown girl! - Little Debbie's distinctions-most unbeknownst, gradually evolved.

On little Debbie Charibert's own part –much by way of inklings how much surrounding horizons though calm, undemonstratively poised broadening, come Monday's long minutes' exploiting possible ways little girl's could effectively dispatch uncompromising construction workers further outside earmarked surroundings, lacked, following graceful thoughts projected over Loving County, Debbie's knowledge proved minimal on extents plausible stories on warrioresses' lakefront consummations spread wildly. All four warrioresses-notably Debbie, aged not one day beyond eleven, functioned alike, disparate opinions others held couldn't matter. Said pursuits possessed insufficient similarities against any such attributes-peers readily frowned upon, accounting leastwise on well-meaning Loving girls still nurturing pure untainted reputations –Each gracious attempts attracting contribution enabling Mentone's improvement must proceed undeterred –boy! -success must derive -No impedance on God's green earth reached high enough, or adequately mustered success preventing oomph, or forestall local folks' eventual admiration.

Outside, thunder rumbled low, spurring morning's pair more spiritedly as assented efforts hashing out points continued.

Dispiritedly, minding many concerned, seasonal rains arrived early, no one-not weather folks associated massive strengths witnessed during most recent downpours --pouring heavily one early morning, thereafter without warning, poured all day, all Mentone regions–including diverse Loving County parts, finally rested underneath flood rising six feet.

This devastatingly acute inability anticipating event correctly, calmed little Debbie's nerves, like many, stood taken aback-quite incapable of thoughtfully accommodating such frightful mishaps any more, or natural disasters as Mentone floods posed equally -as everyone around suffered more, embarrassing countdowns commenced, meanwhile harnessed every last strengths-sticking through relentlessly till final moments as elderly folks say - whatever circumstances prevailed, if another six maybe seven days passes, yet floods hadn't receded, an impromptu rendezvous involving all officially documented warrioresses-whereat more talks on reserved grounds bearing residential blocks ostentatiously decorated using architecture - sorts-speaking edifice-wise, locals beheld pridefully as Loving's own, all one hundred-ninety six regular residents eagerly awaited,

Hours after flood's advent, Debbie seeing water levels all around on streets recede under six inches, exclaimed gleefully as neighbors all around flagrantly defied communicable water borne diseases –wherefore eagerly waded towards directions individual doorsteps led, some rowing shallow canoes thence - managing knee high waters however feasible even if such sights added unprettily upon some seniors' gazing upon frolicking children, or neighbors.

Preceding another day's completion, Debbie's pleasure increased marginally, water levels reduced further below four or five inches, allowing greater locomotion, but on disembarking warm cozy 23 Pecos interiors onto dreary outsides whereat inspect all surroundings constituting Charibert households, little Debbie Charibert discovered ephemerally visual representations far more powerful, bulldozer's looked comparatively insignificant. Mrs. Charibert too gazed upon barring bungalow's main door leading one onto home's first landing; big men, pretty ladies, executive government officials, corporations too as Mr. Charibert informed Debbie later on –Numerous camera operators media houses detailed over, arrived driving big black automobiles around town, modern sorts deemed SUVs, crisscrossed about driving all over town little perturbed by flood levels covering most streets, large rollers these water surfing carriages-almost reached little Debbie's ribcage, rendered flood levels low. Debbie's heart gladdened Charibert's household balcony cradling mother daughter team together, provided relatively distant safety zones - huge rollers moving intrusive vehicles forward proved no threats, not least ones on trucks-most notably one delivery van seen all over town. Sights might have been pretty beholding over twenty cars rigmaroling Mentone, leaving indigenous county folks' proud residents, but underneath sudden visitation during inclement lay disturbing reasons why strangers visited unfamiliar town during present flood season.

These deviated being normal - noted folks: bored prospective land usurpers weren't folks, no local reciprocating kindness ever showed good graces towards land grabbers apparent intentions, ill wishes beside every last one's own's ol' tickers, since set upon deserving treatments as much similar as original hospitalities presented unwanted intruders, Debbie's eleven years living experiences allowed correct guesses - no one hoped acquiring unfamiliar land except sinister motives tally alongside usurpatory tendencies, or possessed disagreeable intents immediate society frowned upon, occupied thinking, however, concerning intruders, pending financial profits mattered more, not local's welfare.   Diverse other heart wrenching thoughts ruminating within, turned out being: moguls resolutely seeking possible avenues seizing any land whatsoever– land, communal land Loving County, most pertinently-Mentone folks inhabited dating right through 1800's till right after days old devastating floods. Now, little Debbie Charibert tackled beyond anyone could effectively handle, disregarding possible outcomes, fixatedly awaited confronting concerns alongside everyone involved.

Hitherto standing alongside younger family observing various automobile kinds roll by, Ayleth Charibert-having retreated inside whereupon attended private matters, reemerged, all wrapped up against chills, immediately observing scenery beside Debbie, but equally wondering practical ways township could taunt passing flood riders through diverse sabotaging deeds-till every single last grabber's spoken word enunciates prayers– *'please, oh–please, grant us hasty departures, Mentone's streets threatens!'* -assailant's hurriedly utter, gearing--local's great rude bangs on overbearing egos-upsetting such fellows' disruptive flows on any upcoming activities - onto being.

Several individuals inside four amidst many cars riding knee high floods, managed friendly waves spectators dotting numerous Pecos street homes entrances or doorways decline returning, like others, Charibert ladies stood huddled amidst themselves amazed as each witnessed events unfolding on water logged streets outside people's homes –ogling Land grabbing water surfers seemed-n't alright, each embodied corrupt politicianhood, or-- even more corrupt bureaucrats Texas whom Debbie certainly understood cherished little or no interest aiding developments around Loving County, let alone Mentone, churned out constantly, though solitary Mentone transcended Debbie's own focus point –entire Loving County besides others soon found out.

As mother daughter near admiration persisted, surrounding road tributaries yielded more cars, joining touring company's already lengthy convoy proceeding close past families spectating.

"We're locals, we mustn't wave drive-bys onward-"

"I thought not, mother,"

"We mustn't arm strangers exploring our destruction, perhaps through courts upon our matters arriving docket - as I envisage, this isn't another trivial matters intermittently probing simple creatures as Mentone's locals, land grabbing's suddenly took on whole new meanings,"

"Mother," Debbie addressed Ayleth, "couldn't we make town's intruders go away, Loving's local's private belongings, land I mean –ought entirely be possessed by local inhabitants!"

Ayleth agreed, issuing following responses,

"I think as well Debbie, but how may we go about attaining such achievements?"

"By redeveloping Loving County real estate lands powerful hard-pressed strangers finds usurpable." Little Debbie's almost spontaneous response encouraged reckonings younger miss Charibert must have started wizening up, many unique aspects showed greater maturity--warranting voicing such deeper thoughts without first mentally resizing words about issuing forth.

"Well Debbie, we'll note eventualities –if our situation meets legal requirements, we'd all visit county court demanding resolutions," -promised Ayleth.

Mrs. Charibert's immediate information rang bells Debbie recognized, young Charibert understood court protocol: administrative buildings aggrieved folks swing by once nowhere else intervenes dwindling personal causes. Ayleth's hopes county courts could stage rescue interventions, made much sense, save one, all others scarcely possessed necessary muscles preventing such prospectors entering anyplace not least Mentone boasting few millionaires controlling much cash, nor influential celebrities, government officials possessing well–? –required. Mentone boasting several– Buchard-Mr. Charibert's Debbie-as on-coming leader, being one, additionally, Buchard currently held several powerful county positions on contract, after disappointments snagging much coveted elected mayor's office –but, if any avails manifest? --Mentone, Loving County, take one's pick --boasted government officials all right, lots amidst locals enjoyed corrupt practices, not least prioritizing personal gains first, society's collective advantages could take distant positions behind—all such issues cared, those without corruption, everyone suspected, refrained publicly, too afraid of voicing revealing thoughts, however, countless past occasions proved many could very well-by choice, raise dissenting voices, soon thereafter, without probable causes affecting private affairs, lost earnest employments, contracts, thereafter, falling on hard times – having little or no respite perceived nigh.

Excepting appropriate preventive activities, shared consensus concur floods possessed hindering capabilities vis-à everyone's progress, not least little Debbie's burgeoning warrioress clique's propositions centered on developing Loving County, however brave, Debbie-never inclined towards allowing herself break, usual approach included first expunging disturbing thoughts as folks stare wide eyed across every street countenancing passage, or across– anywhere whatsoever soon after New Loving breaks Mentone lakefront's sand dunes grounds, mindful of proceeding undeterred, circumstances panning out mattered– if eventually, efforts raise another successful new county, good old little self: could become 'unputdownable' Loving's hot potato -but nicely, making successes result, comparatively cast unfavorable looks on brimming fish kettles– if such mental annotations made any sense.

"Observe us land grabbers –if your lot pleases-" -young miss Charibert taunted passing rogues-almost whisperingly-whilst nestling close by Ayleth - lest one overhear, step out, furiously-charging fists ahead –though assured progressing moments plus neighboring distances typically ensured last vehicle bringing up convoy's rear successfully disappears after others, if only feebly. Instantly as rearmost flood riding automobiles rolled by, objective conclusions gingered Debbie, floods don't always take away areas suiting redevelopment, generally reckoning, floods–do still well-meaning activities, drench vitalities - days, or weeks or months–no more on end, not years, anywhere submerged underneath water reaching one year usually led authorities onto erroneously registering such places disaster zones: ponds-maybe 'creeks', or another strange title generally conferred rolling serpentine waters flowing en-route any set directions-fitting water wading by indifferent ones, or merely represents diversion land grabbers sought delving into.

Back inside, Mrs. Charibert prepared holding Debbie's attention long minutes afterwards discussing– Mrs. Charibert hoped finding out if Debbie's knowledgeableness covered Loving's little girls every town's person touted as county's last hopes erecting Loving County employing many peculiarities - through sand castles-whatsoever. Little Debbie lost already gained apprehensions concerning Ayleth's information passed on moment or two ago, try as much as any possibly, prying eyes failed detecting any preponderances, or preparedness on providing Mrs. Charibert's inquiry touching Mentone's infamous eleven-year-olds any sensible answers; first, Debbie's own personal identity centered on Ayleth's inquiry attested as facts-not rumors were knowledge in tow, meanwhile, little Debbie resisted letting mother have truths, either ladies holding onto varying reasons, needed finding out more.

"May I sit?"

"You will anyhow, dear," Ayleth told, Debbie sat quite agreeingly, "Let's talk dear,"

"Mother–" began little Debbie,

"Yes dear, say, every single matter plaguing your heart?" Ayleth demands set another conversation rolling,

"Any news concerning Lakefront's those little girl's, mother?"

"Arrangements encompassing recreating Loving anew - wielding either sand, perhaps Lego's-as tools, is gathering steam - I hear," Ayleth obviously extending conversation, continued speaking, excepting little Debbie's interruption,

"I see! –dynamic little ones, none I hear condone jokes, no one could ever ridicule young girls toting bright ideas about inside smallish noggins, hearts, minds anymore these days, mom,"

"Yes dear, I absolutely agree,"

"Mother? --heads, hearts, or minds?"

Sensing daughter Debbie sought clarifications, Ayleth Charibert offered Charibert family's eleven-year-old subtle but meaningful understandings,

"Dear, all three work fine, people sometimes have heart-felt ideas, or tote ambitions about inside large or small head regions, others 'mind' obtuse conceptions, others invest minds visualizing variable outlooks possible, any choice; head, heart--should one ever administer usage whilst stressing opinions, often pan out well."

"Mother, Loving welcomes all hospitably during fall, why? --I think father called such prospectors foul appellations last time?"

"We turn nobody away-if one's desires are approaching us peacefully, we haven't malice suffocating our hearts, however, having insinuated mere wishes, flood riders we observed minutes ago, have entrenched deep within each one's heart, greed such as population comprising surrounding localities never experienced –strangers we witnessed drive by are being difficult-Debbie, dear, apprehensions broaden soon enough-I promise, sometimes, one fails resisting powerful attractions overwhelmingly titillating one - over land," Debbie's laughter exposed deep contentment –besides gratitude accorded 'Ayleth': designation Debbie often accredited elder Charibert thoughtwise, forewent questioning interpretations –not least warrioresses' proposed feats known to accentuate many 'powerful attractions' -repeatedly-main topics occupying literary subject matters daughter already attained –whilst craftily excluding character undermining qualifications as 'pushiness' being one, 'wacky' another –boasting months under age eleven, doing situation's best attributing all-encompassing usefulnesses on herself, on Charibert household, or badly stricken Mentone: Texas' small human community, finally Loving County generally, Loving, even if no one recognized lakefront's leading activist as someone pertinent as yet, never mind floods specific whiles back, auscultated little by little through little indecipherable ways–multitudes suggest brought along its own silver lining-submerging all over.

Recent times: two days past-no more– augured disappointingly, however, given endless bustles should new beginnings emerge, formidable advancements flood surfing prospectors driving past front doors reputedly frowned upon, else– assume rank as hometown's domineering little girl - greedy prospectors usually condoned-whilst escaping immediate furies en-route nearest safe havens, but heartfelt presently, or borne within accompanying noggin, perhaps thoughts– as mother divulged –imperatively, maintaining silence typically dissuades Mrs. Charibert; judiciary wig's one half, police captain, Sheriff, not excluding farmer: Debbie's Buchard Charibert duly fit all four descriptions - Loving after all consisted another six towns populated by people subsisting on nether sides but wherein two hundred ought seem humongous during its fullest seasons every accounted person inhabited town, nonetheless sometimes equaled population not beyond twenty two families harboring perpetual intentions over-exerting influence on children, including in motherly ways.

Lone yellow light overhead did justice lighting Charibert's living room as conversations culminating shortly - when Ayleth detailed younger one on county office errands, Ayleth wanted morning's breakfast taken along during Debbie's event delivering lunch, over Debbie's information circumstances warranted simultaneous waterfront visitations; -as Debbie presented dialog concerning Mentone's enterprising Lego or Loving county girls' noting forasmuch as earlier inquiries continued, must burgeon further. Debbie's polite manners elicited quick agreements Mrs. Charibert habitually withheld citing motherly prerogatives, as conflicting household chores clamorously wrestled attention away.

Inside little Debbie's sleep chambers, sorting through wardrobes, several audacious habiliments often worn whenever defiance attitudinizing's justifiably arose, observed ignominy. Less travail threatened confidences today, still- avoided entertaining earnest defiance; mind, or head, or whichever anatomical parts one's creator avowed storage responsibility - exhibiting unreserved readiness folks unwittingly premeditated usurping domineering attitudes those invaders swaggering all over water logged streets not quite an hour ago arrived with; Mentonians, Debbie promised whilst preparations proceeded, contained hard thinkers, wise men forever disapproving stupidities, nearly all professed being patriots emphatically sworn upon protecting Loving county's considerable issues arising; folks knowledge base constantly went with such materialnesses concerning nobody else? -favoring wholehearted decisions Loving requisitely deserved conquering intruders, prospectors, politicians, among additional cohorts: land grabbers, maybe notorious bureaucrats whose corruption engendered continuing indifference, Loving's welfare starting during eighteenth century inception eras-giving Oliver Loving accolades as founder - one evening good graces permitted narrow escape soon after trespassing Indians threatened, but once again reregistered as Loving county, right through present times redevelopment work neared hardest stages, suddenly mattered less.

Mentone folks-once thought hate particularly belonged elsewhere, say– hearts within strangers inhabiting elsewhere–as Ayleth suggested, not Mentone or Loving generally welcoming all, but displeased knowing wading knee deep enroute errand, approaches. Preparing acting presently, additionally, factored influxes constituting wrong kinds-besides ardently casting far reaching aspersions, locals' volte-faced stand caused new perceptions akin Debbie's wisdom - as each gradually grew elder's wisdom, resolving upholding truths inculcated whilst infants however possible.

Soon, wherein ought Debbie prance off but Mickleburgh's, or Chesserbottle's, not Chesserbottle's household next door, but family's small grocery mall one quarter mile away - save through still flooded Mentone terraces? –Little warrioress, convinced Texas should try instituting legislation against such grabbers, given specifically powerful associates, skirted careful ways along treacherous Mentone's saturated street conditions en-route lakefront, several others minding somewhere really important each scheduled attending: places generally subsuming Mentone's local municipal offices, went about wading through knee high waters.

Buchard Charibert's professional rankings as afore mentioned mastering most staff working daily jobs offered by four governmental agencies alongside one privately owned organization, equating superiors variously, held sway, enabling Debbie's mostly galivanting about town, or arriving whenever, wherever ingress gave delights, unchecked until eleven O'clock each morning,

County offices lay sprawling–whereat Debbie encountered burlesque Mr. Helladius Van Linden attending Mayor's office upon-most likely an official invitation preceding engagements involving mandatory talks Buchard Charibert ordered.

Loving's most notorious mogul appeared this morning as per rubbing minds slated recently regarding legal hearing in matters needing hashed over-promised; county judge, sheriff, mayor prosecutor as well, even coroner -all occupied by one person, immediately addressing about renewing Mentone's redevelopment contracts,

"I should think probabilities-if any -success ensues, are slim," one particular county judges resentful on missing Warrioress Lakefront case assignments. Buchard Charibert, first put down an overflowing beer jug, as continuing preparation needed passed on above supposed Helladius Van Linden, seated across, better have, "your fears are well grounded,"

"Why must we treat our children's wishes unaccommodatingly anyhow?" -I should wager-based on my inclination characters behind redevelopment wouldn't decline till success ensues - I'm prepared wagering two hundred quids–" Van Linden, Loving County's most productive, bragged,

"Aren't we union peers? –mm- sir-mister Linden, aren't we?" -argued –Charibert seating back,

"Judge, sheriff--post master-perhaps -these aren't resolute Children, attempting defenestrating old guard." -Van Linden's reduced certainties on allusive titles best befitting Loving county official seated opposite, persisted anyhow, "isn't more uncertainties over our younger ones, immediately highlighting our own folly, failures, shortcomings?" --again needed clarifying intended notions applying suitable words, "during early morning clock-ins, through efforts exerted all working hours until final approvals by appropriate authority, judge, sheriff, postmaster general, whichever expediently suits presently - insomuch as all related duties exit this one desk --I hope being useful if everyone acquiesces."

"I concur," meeting's host agreed joining county offices' dignified visitor's boisterous laughter –Outside, discussion points touched on whilst inside sheriff's office continued as talking point another local patiently awaiting news outside courtroom A-on today's relocated occasion, willfully engaged,

"We have agreement, Aubourc," announced Linden, Linden unpretentiously hoped close-knit groupies immediately comprising amidst members, motherly working girls infusing good measures on greater 'working girls' schemes–known or otherwise, "we have agreement," -moments soon afterwards, dispersed wordlessly all around, gainful confidential pursuits did exist elsewhere one could pursue.

Determination drove Debbie on opposite directions fromwards Beacon Light Lake, providing relief both feet needed against repeat havoc wreaked by second torrential rains pouring down days succeeding initial deluge, exacerbating flood conditions locals already rejoiced receded manageably, levels stayed below even knees locomoting midgets, intending finding out how much damage blueprints already etched on Beacon Light's grounds during last night torrents, hopefully take augmenting steps.

Considering exploits warrioresses staged last time, several stood dismayed Booth's bulldozers still maintained militant presences, but how someone craved obstructing caterpillar's ways-still? –discreet efforts geared actions towards instigating repetitions again, promising exercising greater caution girls next time as caterpillars could irreparably damage little. Deliberate lingering reducingly stacked productive hours onto minutes, ensuring no rivalrous activities commenced, even though hitherto etched New Loving's blueprints tending enduring patiently another few days, remained submerged anyhow, by another forty eight hours, chances were- flood surface alignments recedes below levels permitting visual communications on blueprints embedded atop terra-firma obliging work using blueprints Debbie prayed– like Phoenix rising, help Loving County spring onto greater glories amidst many somewheres' tourists earth-over made perpetual destinations.

Impetuous little Debbie's nature devolved over this troubling matter facing New Loving County-no doubt, since age seven maybe eight –beside school work not least, perhaps Buchard Charibert-perhaps Ayleth, comprised persistent thoughts, little else - day after day, hoping each passing dawn brought hail, hearty supplementing bright arousals-till bedtime-when Mentone ponderings significantly monopolized thoughts all over again.

Regarding water levels on Mentone's Beacon Light lake's sandy beaches covering spots new Loving's blueprints proudly depicted one young senorita's ambitions days ago - sadly, subtle words: if one's spirit holds out, ways attaining success always makes manifest, encouraged Debbie's patience whilst purposively considered manipulating Loving County Council whose affairs frequently occupied all eleven year old Mentonian female children–bar none - however possible; yes indeed, eleven, given Loving's greatly diminished population, plus diversely originated input however minimal, forever dogging, but more importantly, issues concerning minute masses, usually never exceeding twenty people attending local council meetings, plagued exactly by equally limited drudgery, or similarly limiting work protocol entailments, similar departments, as equivalent but comparably staffed offices, throughout Texan counties fortunately staffed by several hundreds' - perchance thousands, even novices understood reasons Loving never grew beyond current status quo.

Once again retraced ways back home underneath still overcast skies wading ankle-deep waters singing melancholic melodies believed uplifted spirits, desperately seeking great outcomes– one day soon, others may very well–due efforts, confer mayor's authorities, an office much older half-brother: Jimmy Wescotte Charibert recently campaigned –perhaps aiming unseating an immediate elder, truth unbeknownst –but given such constant factors usually manifesting as diminished voting, Texas duly appoints succeeding mayors in most cases, family elders.

Decisions approached-though still unpublished; obviously, no ostensible indications showed verdicts gearing towards favoring younger mister Charibert, might have though, supposing Buchard Charibert consented, such unwholesome scenarios renders little difficulties Debbie's crew thitherto faced–though not included within narrative -much easier, as privileges allowed simply sitting alongside potential mayors Chariberts' during suppers, meanwhile spew ideas as denying licenses sought by prospectors like ones rigmaroling all over town this morning - undaunted by floods,

"My! --an idiotic outcome situations'd resemble if father fails securing victory?" -pondered little Debbie thoughtfully, mentally or emotionally as each step brought north 23 Pecos closer convinced craving successes should overwhelm all desirations? –again, not much, successes are all everyone not least Debbie hoped bequeathing drenched Loving, by salvaging everyone's aqueously sunken county, Mentone could once again thrive satisfactorily amidst surrounding counties.

More hearings arrived, either sides remained resolute - refusing altering positions held onto, onliest weapons individual arsenals contained became secret hopes compelling arguments forced Trimble favored side suitably, again Aubourc's expertise as legal counsel, but assisted by Peregrine Hildebald: school teacher tutoring Debbie still– Debbie later learned, lead arguments, by first advising Ticehurst's refrainments prematurely presuming victories - during brief encounters preceding session opening, cleverly employing compendious wording,

"Even accused persons edge near judgment guilt free, remember?" -several unidentified elementary school girls-led by Livilda - entire court furtively observed ceaselessly, pooled by courtroom's rearmost parts, wearing dishonest demeanors interpretations alluded: 'until we ascertain land grabber's identities, we remain relentless', whilst offering retorts during brief greetings as proceeding's commenced, Ticehurst Cholmondeley-charged himself manager overseeing plaintiff's legal affairs surrounding today's hearings, duly cautioned miss Hildebald's awareness-insinuating 'very little comfort,' prosecuting counsel's threats rang clear enough, "remains all- anyone remotely supporting defense collective on prosecution's assigned tasks, should expect."

"We sincerely hope issues never arrives where your oath binds inalterably- if pledges aren't kept," -warned teacher Hildebald.

Today's stillness affecting courtroom atmospheres inundated by locals besides visitors, baffled not least Trimble, somewhere along proceedings, Trimble--habitually uttered straight-faced remarks court room attendees recognized as reflecting heartfelt hospitality, announced time always arrive- instincts dominates reason--not excluding legal matters--If finally prejudice eclipses common sense --great truths indeed!

Defense team led ably by Aubourc's wits abutting miss Peregrine's teacherly discernments, optioned mounting unrelenting lobbyist drives –circumspection many assumed prudent finding more suitable or sophisticated approach beyond working school girl's age-appropriate activities.

THE GREAT ACQUISITION

    Steadfastly possessing several determined ways, little Debbie reached inside Charibert's bungalow-hurrying towards hitting sacks again, holidays alongside vacation abided more, forced on everyone by floods, otherwise, by now, school's new term already coursed along two weeks. Debbie loved schooling, many long treks arriving Bessie Hayne's –like every Mentonian child, felt invigorating, heaping more learning on personal knowledge's repertoire –necessary education evidently needed attaining if great accomplishments occasioned by current personal goals - starting points being Beacon Light's Lego city's sand bound blueprints Bessie Hayne's technical drawing lessons imparted. Debbie continually attained greater convictions of sufficient energy capable of enabling evading disappointments immediately upon projects conception as consequences everyone observed enkindle two essentially overwhelming floods all parts experienced recently.

    Building New Loving-applying mortar clad sand, strategically topped priority, however, considering effortlessness water brimmed broken dykes during or after heightened precipitation over Beacon light, hopes ever getting somewhere merely using sand or mortar diminished greatly: water could simply dismantle sand structures, Consequently, Debbie notionally assumed more ideas; during night's rest, tossing about whilst resting, purposefully immersed within credible thoughts appertaining activities worth any next moves.

    Parental adamancy preventing smart phone permits worsened matters, Ayleth Charibert's stubbornness stiffened citing age-related inappropriateness, unlike most peers, lacked one, otherwise quick summons reaching miss Ravenshield: Livilda, creating awareness over one impending quick rendezvous right after Beacon Light flood recedes – hopefully exposing New Loving's blueprints once again.

    Barely past thinking this, mom's feisty knock shattered evening's stillness followed closely moments later, sounding warnings Livilda's folks accompanied by dearest young Ravenshield friend dropped by. Raising erect onto tired feet, after uttering 'speak about devils…' –not supposing friendly visiting folks equated devilishness–

Debbie's dainty feet carried an almost sleep worsted body after Ayleth Charibert outside, inside bungalow's dimly lit parlor accommodating visiting schoolmate's family awaiting proper welcomes - wondering moodily why Ravenshields chose such inopportune hours. Presently, excited friends hit off invigorating conversation hashing out needless points after unnecessary points covering suitable activities coming next, as mother's, father's on either sides occupied Charibert's living room's far corner discussing, neither girls sitting cozily nearby, quickly considered avoiding madcap approaches when resolving pressing issues given inopportune time, though such social contrivances: little Debbie's departures, augured well, Livilda too bought speaking one's mind entirely, indeed like Debbie, contentious vexations generally facing Loving County as deserving matching competing external Texan counties' standards- as Loving was, like Debbie, obstructions affecting societal onward march mattered very much as well.

Livilda's gallant appearance cladding flowered dress easily out classed Debbie's, leaving good impressions on evening's host-friendly visits lured out of bed, Debbie already rested after day's activities rendering Livilda's fancier dressing tolerable, no one ever really dressed impressively whilst inside personal residences, informed peers excused little Debbie over playing runner-up-vis-à Livilda was concerned on this one occasion sporting peculiar rig outs, otherwise, like young miss Ravenshield, too– prepenses donning on complementary white knee high rain boots, matching flowery dress - colored perhaps another matching hue; alright, making mental notes, promised: '*expect identical dressing next time*', as retaliation next time paying Ravenshield's household unannounced return visits, but wearing much fancier dress lest tattle tales over dressing commence.

Prevalent issues involving reconstructing New Loving, compelled serious arguments often conspiratorially executed through lowered tones parents' keenly observing nearby could not help but detect sisterhood between wards halfway through rearing. Livilda--effectively approving Debbie's leadership: not apropos erecting New Loving - such ideas served Debbie's pride as an original experiment --but about finding solutions resolving Mentone's, by extension Loving county's pressing issues, peerlessly craving resolutions-especially difficult ones, not funfair-like, Debbie could never relent save answers lay underneath numerous sand castle foundations.

On strange whims, young miss Charibert instructed friends Livilda's companionship, without Mrs. Charibert issuing any further permission, Livilda-astern Debbie approaching main doors, shot outside Charibert's, several moments passed, Debbie, forgetful two strengthened feet needed rain boots guaranteeing effective or comfortable locomotion outside; much as Livilda's feet bore one fanciful pair on, much as night clothes should afford warmth, halted, then, retraced steps back inside, thankful over Ayleth's scarcity about. Minutes later, emerged Charibert's household's interiors - feet gratefully clad rain boots, Livilda instantly supposed friend's thickened rubber shoes equated whatever Mentone's outdoors yielded.

"Duty compels I own one," Debbie told Livilda, soon after discuss refocused on smart, or cell phone ownership, progressing any further without having modern devices comprising intended work paraphernalia possessed handily –presumed as impossible, associates needed sustaining constant communications. Warrioresses; designations recently assumed upon many whims, perhaps momentary spurs, left - en-route Livilda's. Upon arriving, Debbie borrowed Skip Ravenshield's most efficient bicycle.

Soon, associates set selves out, meaning reaching Mentone's Odds, bits & ends-thrift store, both intended spending some time browsing store's ostensive leftover knickknacks' collections.

Once browsing shelves containing pre-owned cast-offs, visiting warrioresses agreed on credible choices suiting whom, grabbed one aftermarket Motorola alongside one nearly new though used Apple i-phone; Debbie's - up ahead Livilda's, according enunciated order. Satisfied evening yielded good findings, transferred eager excited selves elsewhere inside town's major general store - initiating fervent haggling.

Already aware certain unknown little girls traversed about exploiting society's sensibilities, counter Lady reminisced days eleven or thereabouts once indicated overall time spent as yet, though visiting pair gave off benignity, immediately suspicious due rumors contents over said entities comprising four little girls –girlhood once passed through, store keeper quickly favored investing curiosity–supporting Beacon light girls efforts furthered by fast-circulating legends, should evening's dyads fit description,

"Those are really modern smart phones dears" evening's customers learned,

"Yes– we are quite aware-miss– business brings us nigh, young females ought have our desired necessities coming here tonight," -little Debbie gazing upon many shimmering objects on sale, addressed Odds & ends shopkeeper, "name prices, affordable prices–please, how much do smart devices cost around here?"

Reducing decibels–preferentially aligning conversation beneath whispers, most tall female of all three released intimate information Debbie standing closest quickly understood perfectly,

"Those? -Take'm, Motorola's, Apples –all are free, as free as breeze we all breathe,"

"Oh?" remarked Livilda, "if my understandings are accurate, we could seize-any desired device, any desired device whatsoever I say, without handing over appropriate premiums, then depart-finding our ways back whence we arrived?"

"Yes dear, free--"

"Very well-Mrs.– but why?"

"Charity– by unknown generous benefactor," Livilda learned,

"Many thanks lady, ah! -plus fellow…" Debbie commenced saying,

"Sagard Summers," Debbie too learned,

"Sagard Summers, mogul, or Admiral gifting working girls good smart communications devices; Admirals--many do duties on ships, military ships I suppose? -Aha! - I see! Sagard Summers work container ships importing Japanese phones?" -inquired Debbie,

"Neither choices Motorola, or Apple, are Japanese, anyways– dears, acknowledged, I'll let Sagard Summers know about appreciation hometown heroines offered," Aubourc spotting broad smiles across carefully beautified face unhesitantly, convinced Debbie mostly willful contribution, as proven countless events previously, taking favorable actions greatly benefited working girl's causes, "but first– each must establish Sprint data plus talk, then text accounts, thereafter purchase air time."

Certainly, neither girls could ever misrecollect parents constantly buying minutes, as each required constantly replenishing usable air time whilst keeping abreast issues, but more importantly, each suspected intensifying interests overwhelming store lady given conversation's gradual direction covering personal interests towards- as evening rather friendly discuss continues, demanding young patrons obtain mother's, maybe father's approvals allowing devices ownership, since either young sisters-apparent subsisted still under-aged minors, next utterances indeed treated concerns similarly,

"Have parents' acceded permissions?" –I must warn, owning these are not only expensive, but require parental approvals--"

"These are no longer smart phones ma'am," retorted Debbie Charibert. Debbie's solitary audience; Livilda being already aware sensibilities queued next Debbie must vocalize -understood, young females could never see previously owned devices as '*smart phones*' -nearly all–on sections behind us, are used phones, even if may yet work wonderfully, used Apples, or Motorola's make calls too –I absolutely don't see why anyone should bother condoning unnecessary protocols disproportionately assigned used items,"

"Then, I won't allow having adults oriented devices, one should not-if avoidable, experience your mother's offensive though righteous indignations, not least poor humble me, later on," replied general store's keeper.

Store matron hadn't significant reasons apportioning fault, Ayleth Charibert, Debbie's mother championed causes involving Mentone's famous 'mother's union' -one tallying seven, chief amongst mantra, 'detesting allowing young preteen daughters' phones: phone easily permit charlatans undue reach on innocent little girls, potentially endangering children, mothers needed looking into every distinctive daughters' involvements till partially eighteen; respecting Debbie Charibert's group et al, eighteen awaited seven years hence - but evidently-too-- tested girls' patience, hence tonight's stealthy appearances underneath Tuesday night's umbra, age eighteen being too far off - no one could possibly wait till age qualification many years permitted owning items everyone else thrived on: but as Debbie determinedly suggested, '*worthless used one*' –hence obligatorily protecting local interested families' interests withholding adult toys' young daughters centered on counter clerk's position. Some sadness did cross benevolent lady's face, imperatively, covert communications needed constant occurrence forthwith between evening's unexpected twain, owning one really, really, really-really mattered very much –particularly duo's dark booted one – as upcoming propositions neared.

Debbie Charibert critically desired perfection helming affairs overpowering ambitions brought on, smart devices appreciably enhanced work companionship facilitating constant connectivity amongst warrioresses –tonight, determination may perhaps ensure privately owned smart device apiece.

"Lady--" argued Debbie, "isn't denying any onward motion whatsoever absurd during these era? –children still won't own devices incontestably guaranteeing interfacing all family members including kids' minute by minute whereabouts due countless ill-informed parents' indignation, every foreseeable circumstance - not mentioning emergencies, considered?" --excuses sufficed easily compelling support,

"Overt sentimentality should never encourage anyone's unquestioning trust on every word another speaks–I know dear, I agree completely, never mind fools --your names-please?"

"Little Debbie Charibert," announced Debbie proudly, "I hereby introduce my friend Livilda, we are working girls - best Mentone, or Loving ever called locals,"

"Aha-! –there they're!" exclaimed storekeeper, making mental connections between past unrelated conversations involving someone citing 'Beacon light girls' as 'Beacon light working girls'.

Little Debbie's wanted succinct knowledge on evaluating most Texas's gimmickry on surrounding legends raised by four Mentone girls-more, perhaps correctly presumed studiously spent time working hard on improving Loving, America's smallest county, one young girl's anticipation heightened each passing day. Abovementioned legends also catalyzed store keeper's general comprehension; somewhere across those six or seven diverse towns mirror'ing Mentone, folks milled about insisting group's choice among considered titles; '*Loving County go-getters*', '*Mentone warrioresses*', '*working girls*' –though peers all through many opportunities, expertly obfuscated description, no attempts intending finding truths through anyone's perceptive abilities would flouris h. Had Aubourc recognized store visitors, no such sympathetic omissions however careless, graces thoughts or action, but, as matters turned out, suspicions gained. Neither girls remotely estimated outcomes situation provided next--

"Working girls--huh?" -inquired wide-eyed merchant lady whereupon moments later smiled broadly, one voluminous shop's patron interpreted realization, engendering store keepers' fondness-

"Yes Mrs.--?"

"I'm Aubourc Shadowbrook," store's already friendly keeper introduced herself,

"Aubourc then– we are working girls, we have important addressable Loving issues," explained Debbie. Beholding one pre-owned 2021 Motorola Edge™ plus disgustfully, yet clutched absolutely tightly any applicable 'repossess laws' couldn't effect reclamation - if mandatory repossession came about, though circumstances remained without conclusively suggesting possible departures owning smart phones honorable, Aubourc's most recent understandings dating back past-few-minutes, solely comprised continuing Loving county's parental prohibition: under aged children must persevere till legal age laws allowed ownership - except one's parents' granted permission.

Debbie fearlessly engaged general store's woman as if lengthy talks mattered: whilst discussions progressed, Debbie made kind but unassuming woman some disclosures owning handsets as great requisites needed by certain sisters out encouraging secretive schemes advancing Loving - if any possibilities existed doing fellow ladies all over one extra favor; insinuations store keeper understood indirectly identified young Mentone duo alongside distinguished waterfront peers, how if eventually matters panned out fine, one more name: belatedly hers: Aubourc Astrid-né Bancroft, stood immense chances rememberable by posterity long afterwards, indeed, here they were- for- Aubourc possessn't daftness which even if traces existed, now perfectly understood nonetheless.

Scarcely having any sensible arguments following little Debbie's words, Aubourc presently informed two patrons working hard on choice device–

"Never worry yourselves, dears, I too, I vow all possible strivings-supporting our own as - working girl, never ever forget!" -thereafter, registered one half million minutes donated lucky recipients by same philanthropist giving away devices, data providers on Apple's, or Motorola's contract also issued on Sagard Summer's behest, once finished, working girls' newest acquaintance solemnly handed each's private properties back.

"Thanks very kindly taking working girl's plight into account, Mrs. -Aubourc," Livilda told stores saleswoman meaningfully, Aubourc beamed knowing younger girls must somehow surreptitiously wish upon openly expressing all emotions, working girls however variously showed most heartfelt gratitude on group's behalf; not long ago, records show duo's sensibilities alike what also impressed one amidst all three ladies inside Shadowbrook & sons. Aubourc beamed, smiles do not exacerbate embarrassments.

Just purchased smart devices already contained ample all-important natively installed two hundred fifty minutes air time, effectively setting Debbie's work balls rolling –Without further ado, much anticipated initiatives kicked off, erecting endless blocks on Beacon Light, somehow proving little Debbie Charibert's worth inside every rumor mill, whilst warrioresses, chief amongst whom, Livilda, lingered close behind.

Sisters hunkered down testing two newly acquired handsets. Exiting store vicinities soon after bidding Aubourc–secretly glad working girls on war path visited under peaceful banners, farewell, one veered left, Debbie, right, instructing selves ahead no less than one hundred yards distance apart could aptly determine devices' workability, whereupon, manipulated every last phone digits assigned each newly acquired working handsets– le-voilà! -like magic, determined pair owned equipment enabling conversations while apart pursuing unrelated businesses, immediately embarked on pursuing disciplines Loving County desperately needed,

"Hello! –am I clearly reaching your earpiece?" -uttered Debbie hollering almost rudely, thank goodness none other stood about else– such's suppositions rudeness just purchased device – unnecessary haste prevented sanitizing - preceding usage, or perhaps not purchased, endured, centered on no one else for chancing about during young girl's phone conversations. Scuff marks filled sets gifted working girls, being vaguely aware attendant telltale scuff marks-previous owner inflicted during enduring usage on 2022 Moto-G bequest, wiped rather firmly on Moto G's surfaces –if being as how bad previous owner's bad breaths lingered on device's mouth pieces still.

"Yes, rather clearly," -Livilda's replies reached back promptly, voice reverberating assuredly inside Debbie's earpiece,

"We're all set, giving prospectors bitter pills reserved intruders, marks our main goals-" remarked Debbie, "by this time next…" -without coherent augmentative remarks furthering ongoing conversation, ideas petered out, however, points made subsumed- putting new timetables on propositions worsened ages ago, moreover, knowing extents diverse factors affected progress; such as more rain, more flooding, or even prairies unusually growing denser, certainly proves difficult considering tender ages eleven, none–except grownups, ever correctly guessed imminent eventuations; keeping fingers crossed, accordingly added whatever unnerved anyone hunkering down on strategically effectuating stoppages.

Equating trigger-happy cowboy gunfighters - by demeanor, little Debbie Charibert leading, Livilda, closest associative chief assistant, following, departed positions young apprehensions moved each towards effecting ownership's all important maiden communications on new handsets, commenced approaching realigning back together on Midland street, contentment shone forth through smiles –much brag-worthy achievements respecting one day's work existed, Mentone's streets rested still underneath ankle-deep waters besides being overcast by deepened umbra.

After bidding farewells till another time, Livilda duly surmised elder Ravenshields must have departed - given incrementally closing Tuesday night hours, mandates parents issued earlier caused parting till another time, Mentone floods receded manageably, or water surfaces no longer impeded society, nor challenged construction workers: working girl warrioresses crew; not bulldozer clad Mr. Emmett Booth or assistants Eardwulf Thornwood most notably could impede onward move evermore.

Home, Debbie met Ayleth finalizing dinner since undergoing preparation.

As usual, nightly meals incorporating steak, Ovaltine: Buchard never slept save some meal accompaniments lent sedation, several inviting bowls brimming scrambled egg, awaiting munching around good company, Mr. Charibert-finally awakened, earnestly prepared dealing evening's late dinner good hands. Mr. & Mrs. Charibert's took usual seating positions-about giving yet another supper good-going moments pending Debbie's re-entrance.

Supper's end permitted Buchard Mr. Charibert's quitting Charibert residences considering scheduled friendly visitations owed certain Mentone friends, leaving Charibert women tending cluttered tables, Debbie, resolute about permanently keeping working equipment bequeathed by one benevolent Sagard Summers through town's general store, beyond Ayleth's knowledge, made starts clearing away dishes, uncertain over mother's willingness on jumping aboard bandwagons if facts covering private propositions, involvements, or purchases–well, till bequests attained discovery. Smart devices usually paid off handsomely-being as how working girl's immediate case needed them, lent much deserved dignity warrioresses craved, hence falsely insinuating proper transactions respecting smart Motorola or Apple devices secured on grounds such facilitated motivations –after all, Mrs. Charibert's permission remained unfeasible, although countless school peers already owned one, particularly few very fortunate ones, those-however inhabited liberal counties thousands strong 'child collectives' commanded great sways, perhaps over ten thousands residing within, accordingly, resulted greater enlightenment beyond capacities any Loving town-not least - Mentone could ever muster, big-city elementary school girls seldom bothered informing parents about intentions obtaining sets anywhere Loving distributed devices –requiring intrepidity one amenable parent allowed, afore one forever disputatious, whilst expecting permits, if such persons subsisted under ages fifteen, ten, or one year ahead Debbie's–twelve, perhaps everywhere else, not conservative Mentone. But subsistence alongside subordinate working girls continued meanwhile wanted more encouragement; no actions anyone hoped taking could ever keep work motivations away now working girls matured onto constant communications; cell, perhaps smart phones nowadays unsubstitutably constituted trade tools hoped bolstered function as; construction worker, chief engineer, or architect responsibly building much rumored up-coming Loving County.

"Mother," started young miss Charibert soon after supper concluded indulgently allowing Charibert women idle away later evening hours, Debbie, though-less idling, ruminated serious thoughts about necessitous undertakings internally, Ayleth Charibert-well occupied knitting expensive wool crochet pieces Mickleburgh's sold recently, or Chesserbottle's, perhaps Cholmondeley's –stale memories wouldn't permit specifics-as all three merchants enjoyed constant Charibert household patronage. Ayleth's demeanor clarified situations, mother needed no interferences presently as Debbie perceived rather great haste mother crucially required - finishing well-made wool cardigan Buchard expected gifted-as token years on end - persevering through various little ways over family's sake. Given perspectives Debbie comprehended Buchard Charibert's position possessing, during recent eavesdropping, most important issues typically paraphrased as, "we shouldn't cut corners working our Loving County, developments, do we?" -good ol' Charibert patriarch, never disavowing support needed by good causes.

Fore-thinking offering whatever available responses, Mrs. Charibert set aside crocheting briefly,

"Dear– take information others forward lightly –grains, salt grains–" Little Debbie understood, much rumor milling around grapevines persisted recently howbeit contained insufficient truths, yet swirl around regularly –news about certain lakefront Warrioresses comfortably matched one such rumors, but contained only partial truths, but not very diversely - parts couldn't piece insinuated ends together, Debbie, associative co-warrioresses-furthermore, though Mrs. Charibert besides all co-warrioresses' parents-too, lacked remotest inklings respective daughters' closely entangled swirling puzzles.

"Mother," begun Debbie snatching up conversation, little caring if Ayleth felt distracted, "mother, do I even remotely seem like one amongst warrioresses heard about?"

Mrs. Charibert laughed almost inaudibly, Ayleth thoroughly failed envisioning possibilities little Debbie made list as one budding feisty little thing shaking Mentone up with waves emerging rumor mills, Ayleth immediately let Charibert child apprehend personal positions,

"Be sensible Debbie," Mrs. Charibert warned–widened smiles replacing one already domineering visages,

"I do not see how– Debbie my daughter could ever toe those girl's lines, no one ever hears greater decibels beyond joyous tones around my dear daughter, moreover, your father ranks amidst most conservative individuals inhabiting Texas cities, notoriously unsympathetic towards such illicit pursuits,"

Fundamentally, Mrs. Charibert appeared as one about condemning or showing distaste-should daughter ever link up warrioresses activities, motherly duties sometimes encompassed providing good opinions, though little by character's way indicated any qualifications remotely associating daughter Debbie amongst such feisty waterfront bundles one expects led massive riots-everybody Mentonian believed soon, over rumored new County construction rather than improving existing ones. Mrs. Charibert maintained certain discrepant explanations, such attitudes weren't usually any attributes identifiably Chariberts',

"Debbie, one requires best deals worlds offer," -Debbie quickly interrupted Ayleth, Debbie anticipated Ayleth–furnishing more clarification inherent within- '*both worlds*' best– symbolized,

"Best– worlds?" -intoned Debbie pensively,

Mrs. Charibert understood daughter Debbie's loss, such seldomly used expression often carried deeper meanings beyond psyches eleven year olds mustered,

"I mean, really wealthy folks –possessing expendable tons enabling one garner authority, subsequently, influence others,"

"I see!" -agreed Debbie - mentally searching analyzing preferred wordings subsequent conversation must relay, "mother, I suppose rich folks? -no?"

"Rich folks, Debbie, rich folks."

"Agreed,"

Accordingly, Debbie let evening's overriding topic rest, pursuing treated topics any further terribly wasted precious moments, if Mrs. Charibert–one-amidst all humanity Debbie believed should possess most knowledge about daughter's capabilities, sounded profoundly dismissive,

"Debbie, I am your mother, I know all your adventures, including those little crushes–"

"Ma–" -little Debbie readied complaining, but Ayleth Mrs. Charibert apparently held more arguments awaiting spewing forth, resultingly, held back whilst mother essentially- found fun picking young miss Charibert's brains, Debbie most notably, increasingly perfected through aging, though not yet skilled, sustaining protracted conversations still posed little botherations, however, fared well enough, later situations may perhaps encourage more if attitudes—or alterations thereof, permits closer interactions,

"Debbie, I do empathize, but first, try much more verbal entertainment, similar circumstances spanning recent times apropos your comportment, show lack thereof, moreover, comparably, all blonde girls are not crazed as disaffected legends suggest."

'*Subtle words wise ones hanker after*'; thought Debbie smoothing gold blonde hair clad forever as now wearing gold tiara - agreeing, not all blonde girls bear conceal indecorousness, although, Debbie neither comprehended nor accepted - spotting blonde locks synonymously close by craziness, all continuing efforts hinted on, entailed county wide patriotism.

Within Ayleth's words-insinuating understanding confusion, little Debbie Charibert deciphered mother's general approval insofar as continuing whatever good proposals any young daughter harbored within, heart or head, suddenly meant very much, Debbie thenceforwards voiced herself - but also Mrs. Charibert most solemn oaths, though none verbal communication; rest'll never occur until pertaining talk became prominent amongst reasons Loving County folks gossiped.

BLENDING WITH THE SHADOWS

Situation warranted twenty-four hours passing - permitting individual focuses merging back on themselves, however, scarcely outside moments folks hung beyond earshot, or out visiting someone, concerning Debbie's case - often showing guests sleep chambers Chariberts visitors often passed nights, as telephone conversation hideouts--Mrs. Charibert left unlocked suiting today's telephone event. Moments after locating Ayleth's key depot, seized one relevant bunch, inserted one appropriate one inside key fissures, brief moments later, witnessed locks unfasten, yielding outsides, Ravenshield's held similar situations: Livilda-accessing family rush room, or one situated right inside private sleep chambers, facilitated inaudibility, obscuring unfinished conversations participants wanted away from anyone's knowledge.

Lots ruminated within Debbie's head, or mind, or heart on approaching telephone conversations -though not certain since precise comprehension still required ascertaining –one being considerations touching on going underground, Livilda's inquiries-if 'underground' signified some other valuable meanings, Debbie's dialogue during following explanations, though unvoiced within narratives ensued.

Monday morning dawned, bringing along many joyfulnesses– high flying girls arrived school on time whereon, met other school children natively nearby towns', parts or counties - attending school, everyone scurried about joyfully knowing boundless introspections each bore, cooled off during busy weekend activities, but Monday also brought along more tedious learning opportunities, as agreed-upon arriving schoolwork qualified tackling first, class work duly commenced.

While Debbie properly addressed few girls one on one, Livilda served others entertaining talks about new club's invitations accommodating good girls whose parents proudly brandished, causing peer families great envy over good girls virtuously upholding expected proprieties. Debbie sat erect busying herself informing peers interestedly awaiting serious sermons cueing any imminent communication: how time subsequently arrived everyone; themselves, peers, teachers, even parents, must ginger behaviors up, stressing imperativeness of making strenuous efforts once families across Loving country welcome convictions good support always bided good: those girls touted 'mastery of Beacon Lake waterfront' harbored up skinny sleeves, given personal perspectives additionally-co-warrioresses' every nagging viewpoints, whatever on going attempts-circulating furiously within grapevines beforehand, must forebode good.

Debbie's classmates went without naiveté, while selflessly supporting good causes lit by one peer, though upon inquiry, posthaste responses conveying little Debbie Charibert's truthless replies denying involvement, reached all however, promised helping find out girls' exact identities thereafter, return comprehensive reports everyone wishes upon.

Several female peers quartered alongside Debbie's Bessie Haynes' B class, demanded Debbie disclose related benefits awaiting enlistees - should any decide lending support-doing exactly as pledges not quite one minute insinuated, various others hoped learning reasons taking on matters assumed Debbie's personal issues, sundry pupils demanded knowing outright if loudly touted warrior girls contained any Debbie's unidentified relatives, leaving Debbie immediately making insightful inquiries,

"Don't mind if I am," ensued quick retorts just as another question sounded, "do I little Debbie Charibert, appear 'waterfront girl-likely?" -none about retained any offerable responses suiting peer's inquiry uttered just now, non-however thought otherwise, but more importantly, non-insisted positively, instituting even keels, not leaning hither, nor thither-given peer's collective estimations.

Upon several minutes' passage, every B classroom female pupil pledged unwavering complicity waterfront ladies needed desperately through Debbie Charibert, most wished classroom's appreciation reserved idolized warrioresses duly reached girls involved, every Loving schoolgirl's support heaped boundlessly awaiting implied one's enjoyment-apropos whatever endeavors occupied ring's fancy, provided occupations checked out good, B girls promised informing parents-pledging doing whatever could possibly help lure widespread parental support over even if by by inveiglement means.

Several amidst noted young Loving ladies negotiating through preadolescence years underneath fathers holding similar posts as Buchard Charibert, but thereat distant parts, such as; police Commissioner, police captain, sheriff, judge-or chief judge, perhaps coroner, accorded various indications of diversely choice'd lingos suggesting Loving'd suffered enough diminutiveness, again, recommended-if Loving wanted co-equal status among counties, better rise off its haunches.

Needless saying, not one possessed proper comprehension as respects real messages implicit within utterances, inasmuch as local population never topped two hundred twenty during any periods, accordingly, enable residential hopefuls continuous influx, maybe overwhelm Loving, houses needed constructing, roads infrastructure permitting locomotion between one county's point's en-route others should population increase by as much or as little as 5% depending individual knowledge based accessed, too. Firm promises issued all around promoted relaxed moods since Debbie longed letting all morning activities excepting regulation allowing teachers take turns delivering lessons, slide - glad much accomplished successfully.

Recess periods saw clique's newest associates: Victoria, Loving's crude resources mogul-Helladius Van Linden's last child, exclusively known amid all primary school pupils studying Bessie Haynes elementary classes as onliest elementary age pupil permitted smart phone usage by father: Helladius Van Linden, hung close as discussions continued, neglecting appetites urging quick feasting inside Bessie Haynes student's refectory.

During pertinent discussion observed by schoolmates as enterprising doublet stood abreast one another during utterances verbalizing Victoria's unreserved support inveigling Van Linden enterprises' unwavering support touching Beacon Light endeavors, titbits gossips contained whereas school pupils witnessed another friendship as well as talks warrioresses assayed functioning constantly as faceless little girls, blossoming, thereafter reached Debbie's ears. As school children located individual schoolroom-given ceaselessly summoning school bells, Miss Van Linden's made flattering entreaties requesting Debbie's assistance with half opportunities upon which effect introductions between all - 'those' girls inclusive, prior parting, stated much gratitude finally meeting someone like Miss Charibert's person acceptable as real-world role model, received solemn promises evocating no less. Following Debbie's mental appraisals giving Victoria pass marks as potential warrioress, vowed doing everything potentially possible Victoria Van Linden personally encounters all waterfront's enterprising girls. Debbie indicated enforcing meetings before long, Debbie tried soothing Victoria's unvoiced fears-foregoing's might demonstrably prove one amid numerous fraudulent means reprobates rustle finances –submitting Victoria's guarantors ought set aside any fears, become rest assured initiative went without worries, but first reeled off plenty appreciations,

"Bless your heart Victoria-" gratified warrioresses about voiced harmoniously, as opted Debbie followingly- "words could never express satisfaction having someone worthy alongside efforts imbues us," -Debbie proudly announced, "here's my broad smile honoring your support." Smiling broadly as hinted partly constituted next logical actions, "we do welcome your assistance," -thenceforward. After severally exchanging heartfelt vows professing commitment, delighted, all reestablished classroom presences –after managing raising just few farthings self-donations as New Loving's initial capital mustered during past few months, on carefulness's account, Debbie secretly dreaded potentially sassy Miss Van Linden remarks: *save my help-who else possesses such initial working-girl's working capital.*

School day ended soon enough, one very determined Debbie, accompanied by another equally motivated one, Livilda, walked gallantly facing directions family houses situated, feeling elated assuming positions amongst mobile little girls occupying smart phones savvy ranks, chatted between themselves as dainty steps continually encouraged each towards personal residence's general directions, reacquainting folks with selves suddenly cut ice, each- proud momentum gradually increased gainful admissions, more willing associates desired joining, several-projecting firm promises individual parents owned enough liquidity warrioresses may well seize pronto - not later than one day past dates originally anticipated finances arrived by truckloads - if going by fantasies–

"Understood," replied Livilda,

"Look! -exceedingly magical I say! -without much hesitation, Miss Linden reached someone confidentially via private handset's second line as we conversed-" –Victoria's comments preceding switching phone lines included; "Debbie, cash's one important feature none of us considered yet," boom! -several minutes later, obtained valuable cash pledged during conversation held across lines reaching some someone somewhere–

"Yes, warrioresses're going places, don't ever forget-" warned Livilda happily,

"Indeed, how could I?" retorted Debbie,

"Two thousand quid! –oh!-my! enough money one could purchase multiple everything,"

"Can't really judge books by cover jackets, mother says often," sounded surprised Livilda sincerely overjoyed school most prominent girl's obvious interest anent 'warrioresses' situation, "look! –Victoria? –astonishing!"

"Yes, Victoria, whom I suppose possesses plenty promise, really, our onliest hope as warrioresses going forward, if I could ever sound convincing, perhaps, joining our ranks could result, we'd all proudly go about dissimilar businesses," --School bags strapped on back sides, more conversation ensued through smart phones pressed hard down on attentive ears, inexplicably hurried homewards - making strenuous efforts busy feet avoided accidentally stepping against puddle lining Mentone streets till Pecos.

*   *   *

Friday morning skies brought entire Mentone–perhaps remaining Loving County greater ease, Debbie, toting comprehensive lists - counting Livilda, Camilla, Isabella-Zoe additionally, arrived work zone now rumored as- '*Phoenix rising encore edition.*

Flood once submerged Beacon Lake, obfuscating lake levels but thankfully, receded far beneath earth's surface, all sunken, lastingly wetting Loving's earth, painfully erasing Debbie's blueprints drawn on Mentone's terra-firma portrayed bare once again. '*But, do not worry,*' Debbie's self-consolation caused an unintended smile, redrawing blueprints needed minimal efforts, moreover, reckoned erasure might yet betide working girls as one welcome event, since redrawing another, antecedently designed blueprints removed by flood waters stood greater chances of advancing.

"Ladies," Debbie took on warrioresses, "come Monday next, hereupon our feet rest, shall our starting points dwell- making changes Loving deserve, we needn't always talk ourselves silly without deeds, we need act more effective now– we must speak more –between ourselves no less, till any more arguments, none but ourselves know four warrioresses's identities," -pausing briefly whilst breath filled out wheezy lungs, compelled herself onto continuation, "I say-rolling balls rest underneath our feet, similar events happen once during life times, great hearted someone's: ourselves, retaining great big obtrusive ideas no one ever ignores once taken shape, I'm confident," Debbie Charibert paused awhile, but endured further, "I should not pretend our move represents world's best activity since mister –'*mister whomever*', invented sliced bread, bringing Loving-nation's brash attention - even bold reprisals, covering laudable pursuits advancing Loving society, Loving ought feel like counties elsewhere," -pausing, then breathing severally, given warranted continuations, spoke more, "-new Loving must rise under duress exerted by willing participants."

Much concurrence abounded amidst Debbie's small audience, attendant peers friends searched, but found little justifications refusing or engaging talks –just proffered arguments made perfect sense, moreover, tangoing often took two-if sayings prove any worth, as regards pertinent discuss, subsisting alongside Debbie Charibert if any implicit aspirations assumes corporeal status, was requirements, none needed adopting nationalistic attitudes - holed up inside small town Mentone, verily appreciating renown all over elsewhere, little by little -goodness surrounding warrioresses' reputation enhanced more, designations: '*Mentone warrioresses*' on every lips, threatened outmatching most valued county staff's.

Barring certain hardy but childish Mentone female children, everyone clamorously fought over little female warrioress' gang's membership affiliations or enlistments, still, none could boast visually recognizing any Mentone daughter involved, as yet, identities remained outside perturbing issue plaguing Loving or any surrounding small towns couldn't tolerate, or without, authorities' not detecting any constitutional disobedience regarding local laws or ordinances calmed government officials-though local parents themselves; viewing matters through greater perspective, inside Loving holding one hundred-sixty two, not beyond one hundred ninety, maybe fewer, principally comprising figures beneath twenty two families, every major office featured someone resident families allocated government, although increasingly across contemporary times, few none locals successfully gained offices local Mentonian's once permanently manned - by adept social elbowing, one fad increasingly taking root within Loving county, Debbie remained bewildered wanting proper christenable monikers residents deserved, numerous efforts converged onto deciding on one anyhow -All hopes geared towards finding self-provisional solutions one day soon, but firstly, best collective epithets most suitable, persisting mindfully read; Lovingers, or Lovians, or appellations akin, but, designating suitably-too - issues deserving further strife another time: indignations justifying myriad brainless individuals intending on moving back, hoping such migration demonstrates appreciation, after all, coining inhabitants relocating back, two acceptable monikers, else--

Mostly puzzlements observed practically deriving within everyone sorting out stories about exciting young daughters Beacon light gave– or about given chances, heavy equipment drivers assigned construction vehicles-many later realized, expertly conducted most circulating rumor mongering Cholmondeleys' ever hosted, solitarily posited inn one Ticehurst Cholmondeley founded on sleazy tokens one dreary morning hoping downcast strangers as local fellows'd find hope partaking grapevine's fruits -but upon patronizing business Cholmondeley's openly offered people obsessedly milled more rumors; opinions concerning 'working girls', centered more amongst all topics hashed out anywhere, or intermittently restarting previously hashed out issues, if gathering's continuity must feel appropriate or within reason's vestiges over whatever continuing warrioresses' arguments rooted deeply within people's memories, despite beliefs, such little dented working girls burgeoning reputation, rather, even if all unfavorable arguments insisted warrioresses charading too much nosiness:- sort no one felt comfortable 'liking' –as no known person residing Loving currently, lived without secret hopes 'daughter', or plural thereof, successfully enlisted Beacon Light's working girls, still, Mentone parents duly felt needs keeping keen eyes on daughters waterfront girls--no doubt personified, as indicatively, such comprised sorts lured off by strange places when adults, never again reinstating Loving roots --by carefully articulated words, folks hoped keeping daughters permanent Loving locals ensuring hometown's continued good legacies, perhaps like most secretly ascribed 'working girls' current activities.

However-much everyone openly bought pitched arguments: Beacon Light girls; whomever made group's statistics, needed concerning themselves being little girls, not obstructing construction workers deploying tact quibbling hard hatted fellow's reportage everyone bought - as being an exclusive experience whilst endeavor's initial stages progressed gradually.

Few short minutes after commencement, morning's lakefront meeting reached termination –foregone conclusions– lakefront qualified as New Loving deserving prime locations little fun seekers gathered during early evenings, strolled along well laid beaches-accoutering fancy dresses, or everyone reposed thereat soaking up sea breezes as sun bathing beach goers immodestly descry ingress inland, but envisaging as oceanfront emanating sea breezes ushering chills - temporarily suppressing entire Loving constant worries, never before hitting such accuracies, helped matters tremendously:

"Next rendezvous girls--" expressed Debbie as each girl prepared re-acquainting themselves with individual abodes –as all took first few departing steps towards directions opposite ones four others headed, Debbie, noticeably impatient, fished out one recently gifted Motorola-whereupon conversation commenced, Livilda manning opposite lines ensued, naturally, Livilda's proved one phone digits immediately accessible, another - Victoria's; visionary twain's initial reluctance satisfying Isabella's or Camilla's or Zoe's curiosities over recent hardware investments making such necessary acquisitions: communication tools Sagard Summer's distributor supplied, somehow established 'inner circles, or within gang, though, yet another issue arguable another time - as all three girls possessed debilitating indifference or trustingness on forebears ways, little effort or time one required mishandling intermingling events inside individual homes help divulge unauthorized smart device's ownership should anyone involved enable peers acquire free phones much as Debbie led Livilda onto accomplishing - not quite seven days.

Gadarene steps demoed by three accompanying girls: Camilla, Isabella, alongside Zoe, convinced Debbie wrong choices may yet have been made appointing each objectionable member: pacing hard, obviously failed suppressing departure haste, this Debbie brought Livilda's attention. Livilda too noticing homeward bound trio hurrying away rapidly, deemed uncharacteristic hasty departures-immaturity, gang's second person simply positioned beside Debbie tailed everywhere by warrioresses' second trio-forever succeeding first group comprising; Debbie, Victoria, then Livilda: Camilla, Isabella, besides Zoe -better luck next time apportioning strange untried peers drive activities, Debbie could reliably expect firm–complementary working girl's efforts until project's termination –Notwithstanding circumstances, managed prying out promises- minding prevailing knife edge uncertainties about envisaged situations, accordingly never reveal working girl's identities never mind interested parties inquiring - not even concerned parents, nor sisters, no fellow elementary school pupil, conceding suchlike, greatly enhanced invulnerabilities duty bound respective 'warrioresses' alongside all Loving's general population, all three acceded. Debbie instinctively apprehended great departure hurries, as signaling those three's lackluster interests, New Loving's blueprints appearing uninspirational, also discouraged several more, however starting immediately, collectedly prepped proceeding alone without assistance should Livilda-maybe Victoria-too-drop out eventually. Miss Van Linden's through continuing circumstance's second Apple's earpiece, insisted much agreement, Debbie's idea ticked fancies, apparent truths contained within self-explained plots hence an almost spontaneous thousand dollars' donations, Victoria posting absences mattered little, many such occasions cued passing related events –whomever lurked behind humongous donations, as Helladius Van Linden, although often generously gifting children latest smart technologies, obviously bordered enlightenment theories allowing daughters away indefinitely, appointing chauffeurs alongside personal assistant duly obligated oversight duties on every warrioresses' newest member's moves, like warrioresses' senior duo, clocked eleven as well --Debbie understood, but presences counted little, or much, though not very, Van Linden's redeemable pledge provided working capital through contributions: two or four thousands naturally, but mostly exclusively weighed onto greater considerations. V i c t o r i a again asked Debbie apart, explicit information chief working girl must have vitally wanted immediate disclosure, promised grants awaited warrioress' personally operated checking account remittances, accounts serving group as safe haven awaiting incoming thousands - amounting over twenty.

Somewhat afraid inadvertently speaking inadequate thanks - given such huge sum bequeathed by Victoria though reserved for onward bank transmittal, unceasing awe compelled Debbie's inquisitions- perhaps scarcity thereof, obligatorily forced poor Mr. Van Linden's massive amount's departure from personal coffers, Victoria's simple reply consisted own's insistence on receiving quick funds facilitating modern clothing purchase - likes every Bessie Haynes' schoolchild pridefully flaunted these days –Van Linden thus felt obligated committing resources, forthwith– decided making provisioned monies -family's personal donation headed much talked about working girls-whomever made up rank's -ways.

Quite acceptable-surrounding families offering donations, Debbie found no more reasons doubting Miss Van Linden beyond this, commonly circulated legend postulated no further known individuals dealing crude commanded more influence, success or money as did Victoria's family, whence four thousands parted ways without so much as query why, such sultry thousand sums, thereupon - so- proved little botheration, Van Linden's wasted no second thoughts tossing four away.

On inquiry covering suitable manners transferring working girls capital essentially required, Debbie resisted immediately receiving funds, scared stiff named amounts reached humongouity, after all among work arsenals included one working smart phone admittedly paid one sultry price unaffected by cost - minding situations ten dollars amounted exorbitant cash an eleven year old assigned personal trappings, managing four thousands cash attending one's whereabouts seemed undoable, such huge sum immediately distract small children's adherences: sensibilities following morals parent's continually taught, wither, focusing on all proper problem solving approaches suffer as well.

Debbie's understanding why most officials entrusted large sums, are sooner–some later arrested, embezzlement being main charges; controlling thousands money denomination dollars seemed unmanageable, money immediately permeated extravagancy throughout Debbie's thought processes, buying fancy dresses if ever spare changes remained - no matter assuagements awaited such earmarked monies'; purchasing other stuff like brand new modern smart device inholding multiple communications lines–fully suiting simultaneous conversation occurring frequently, amongst several warrioresses, accompanied these splurge oriented thoughts, Debbie pleadingly recommended Victoria ensure stowing warrioresses working capital inside one personal account four thousand dollars currently reposed, suggesting consultations, each involved reckoned benefits existed finding suitable timetables forsaking unwarranted corrupting ideas.

Victoria's smile denoted satisfaction, realization-sinister jests brewed perhaps elsewhere, not underneath current matter, Debbie indeed appeared dithering on ridiculing gullible peer(s) - perhaps due unchecked kindnesses, or willfully contributing whatever possible efforts Beacon Light critically anticipated encountering wants of, by siphoning feasibly funds numerous sources donated, by insisting original source maintain sole authority dispensing gang's income, Debbie veritably proved honesty, no– indeed, sinister gambits cleverly omitted fraudulent attempts, Miss Van Linden trusted Debbie even more afterwards following Debbie's recommendation, through telephone dialog conducted stealthily folks could never overhear as implausibly explaining true financial source or sources, several little lies mish-mashing facts should adequately explain situation should Mrs. Charibert discover innocent Debbie master-minding mission's diligences.

Following agreements Victoria meet persons charged warrioresses bursary operation's-if Debbie attended, satisfied all optimistic affectations setting aside fears concerning personal assistant's motives, smoothed nerves: Victoria, indubitably increasingly committing efforts, apparent. Affirmatively agreed meeting Victoria, Debbie entertained certain fears about making group's new promising rich girl an assistant, till earlier on today, no one encourages contemplating fear –excepting such persons owned amounts exceeding many thousands --warranting caution once such person functions about; drawing inspiration an unrelated narrative Mrs. Charibert once discussed engendered; how four thousands reached beyond negligible sums one totes about on one's person despite owning great wealth or being socially positioned, except irresponsible, arguing thousands-however few, amounted to-n't nearly enough random strangers'd make detours once awareness someone nearby shifted-about carrying huge sums, else immediately adopt roguish methods-coming after one, asserting further, stated such money equivalents sufficed purchasing plenty valuables Charibert's household certainly wished holding, suggesting Debbie ought pray young girls never encountered such overwhelming amounts unguarded lest collapsing onto one hapless heap atop hard cement floors crying, occur, thereafter, cede one's-self under police arrest-contemplating '*possessing illegal amounts*' charges, as constabularies all over Loving County usually pined endlessly finding huge currency's sources. Whilst Debbie's immediate objectives besides crying over greatly diminished financial shortages, also encompassed not allowing authorities discover someone, none exclusive- bearing inexplicable amounts –ventured making further agreements Victoria's ever-present entourage found acceptable; all mentally assessed joints club girl's often assemble frequently once hour clocks 7 PM for next day's evening's rendezvous during dusk. Debbie reckoning Mrs. Charibert already augmented evening meal decisions intending ordering refried bean cans as main course during supper, Mentone's grocery stores most probably Chesserbottle's, but also Mickleburgh's, offered those, quickly factored in diverse itineraries–

Sustaining cheers, all sides declared today's events lent worth on anticipated repeat rendezvous, shortly afterward ended progressing telephone conversation.

Joyous dreams manifested finally as ambitions kicked off, warrioresses desired forthwith every supply building New Loving all interested Lovingers or Lovians could reside pridefully going ahead - required. Days traversed humankind as usual, though much slowly in comparison, bringing along realizations why Ayleth Charibert once held unflinching opinions - each time anyone expected any good, or success got going, time comes conniving, if any good approached, or as current discuss' stipulates– going; much good approached suffusing working-girls drive members observed increasingly hungered after every dime obtainable by Loving county's most preeminent family-responsibly answering one member peer's supplications with great dollar donations.

Debbie's siesta lasted ages, but suddenly, strange noises caused jolted reawakening, Omega's most archaic clocks situated on an IKEA dresser adorning bed's lower ends, showed multiple hours passed during times dozing, time read 8:45 O'clock PM. Great anticipations Debbie grappled ongoingly, not tomorrow morning, nor evening, but right this very moment.

By great benedictions, next Debbie's eyelids flickered open, morning shone bright, several story books ensured sleep took away many worries, Debbie's fixated gaze upon another wall hung old Omega, times shown told Debbie morning's activities cued once again. Feeling refreshed, Mentone's self-made heroine struggled up, put on aging bath shoes depressed onto one side by many usages, like Ayleth instructed years ago, excused herself, situation warranted dropping by room seven - housing one particular Charibert's household baths, making reappearances after exact time Ayleth advised spending bathing.

Ample time later, little Debbie Charibert reappeared, all dressed up suiting day's activities, thankfully, Saturday-first weekend day, progressed gingerly giving none sufficient grounds accessing school hurriedly, rendering matters much easier, bearing naught else-but Loving? –as constant preoccupation within one young burgeoning mind, or heart, or head, however, herewith, Debbie's belief one's mind held worries more particularly suddenly looked more accurate.

UNEXPLAINED DISAPPEARANCES

7 PM on appointed time, Debbie prepared sauntering off, Beacon Light beckoned, upon arrival, several unrecognizable near strangers accompanied about by short statures indicating persons not beyond ten or eleven, due surrounding darkness, identities remained indeterminate after initial glance, or many later, filled one frightened vision; barring figures being midgets someone recruited during groups formative process--busy accompanying Victoria here, thereafter, another rendezvous Victoria approved, passed off smoothly – till yet another summit thereabouts twenty four hours hence.

Such encounters took after much unlikeness anyhow, people as fascinating as midgets seldom interfered anywhere let alone warrioresses activities.

Next day's afternoon progress carried through smoothly, bringing along supper, Mrs. Charibert knowing Buchard Mr. Charibert expected hearty meals each evening, informed Debbie certain scarce items justified leaving 23 Pecos confines right away, Chesserbottle's or Mickleburgh's near town's busiest points measuring exactly four hundred yards beyond Chariberts', stocked Hormel's red bean cans whence many previous purchases occurred, Mickleburgh's store keepers accustomed thoughts erroneously often mistaking every appearance as bean can errand, but come 5 PM, Mrs. Charibert's voice summoning Debbie kitchen-ward remained still - ungracing Debbie's auditory nerves, however, moments later, Ayleth's voice, easily shattering early evening's stillness, summoned Debbie. Upon reaching Ayleth hurriedly, announcements conveying urgent groceries errands purchasing bean can or two, almost startled Debbie; all day passed whilst Debbie awaited mother's audacious summons. Darkened minutes past five meridians, these representing another meteorological season heralding shorter days after longer nights, hence five medians already posed darkness --however altered circumstances; Ayleth's almost unpleasant voice called - summoning ward out instantly, scheduled errands needed urgent attendance, past discussions invariably established evening errand entailing visiting several Mentone's groceries, aforementioned outing cost good timing whilst attempts continued perfectly aligning evening's pending scenarios, Debbie premeditated detouring Beacon Light's routes, either whilst approaching or departing scheduled meetings, once concluded, dedicate herself eating supper.

Passage through front doors passed without salutatory bidding invariably establishing Ayleth's need for haste. Once inside unwelcoming umbriferous outsides, marched en-route waterfront. Thankfully, evening's stillness posed little or no difficulties that soon, quick steps placed bean can messenger onto trek's terminus. Here as anticipated, beheld small human images shaded behind shadows all over again, each no taller, ordinarily, spooky sights left little girls–not Debbie, afeard.

"Sshh-!" Debbie heard lowered voices desperately attempting attracting attention through quiet decibels night's age-old 'silence' ordinances demanded. Perceiving sound must have been someone's voice, or voices peculiarly small peoples' lurking behind shadows, listened more keenly, indeed familiar voices - one anyhow, sounded forth yet again, upon keener listening, reckoned Livilda's.

Smiling due greater reassurance, Debbie approached nearest shadows presumed Livilda's, relief routed rising trepidations once presumptions proved true.

"Hello folks," saluted Debbie-in fashion reminiscent on Ayleth's once encountering associates upon reaching Livilda's side by four others, "how come trepidations scarcely shows about being here this hour?"

"Evening, Debbie, now's definitely evening," -evening periods-atmospheres truly indicated all around –one not yet night-time anyhow, but gladly accepted co-warrioresses corrections.

"Oh, man!" began Debbie hoping instigations enabling speech, called forth proper conversation, "I admire your courage hanging out here alone."

"Debbie, everyone guesses right over good coming our way, we're here awaiting Ms. Van Linden, Miss Linden has--as I heard, useful goodies offered us,"

"Certainly, we discussed obtainable goodies earlier on, hadn't we?

"Right –indeed Debbie, I'm sure Victoria'll attend soon, no one all through childhood days associates new girl with regretful attitudes as reneging on promises."

Debbie's words made manifest moments later as illuminated beams preceding - as Debbie et aliae discovered later on, an expensive automobile turned corners, briefly exposing snug positions within surrounding umbra, subsequent moments revealed all three flustered-instinctively undertaking evasive maneuvers, realization bright bathing lights shone fleetingly as eagerly as moments thereafter when headlights swerved away, Mentone's almost suffocating darkness once again enveloped surroundings, saving peers any more embarrassments.

Presently, Victoria's chauffeur driven carriage pulled up alongside working girls huddled together, out alighted special guest clutching two school bags spectators swore contained surpluses none correctly guessed seven yards away.

Evening's balminess caused cold shivers, though-truthfully speaking, needed far more bite on anyone holding dead set positions against participating outdoor activities upon inopportune hour - granted Debbie's situation, flew by quickly, Debbie confidently desired succeeding events followed tout de suite.

Debbie's warrioresses leadership remained intact-earning more validation by Victoria breezing past Livilda standing erect by another compeer, though– attitude quite omitted daring rudeness, like all three, longings now remained briskly finishing present occupations, ensuingly, swiftly rekindle family's closeness. Dauntless against further delays, discussions progressed-through low tones lowered below any appreciable sonance, mandatorily, Debbie took discreetness seriously, moreover, interlocutors' personal perspectives requisitely mandated exercising utmost caution.

"I have my pledges I must deliver presently," announced Victoria, an announcement waiting could have perceived light up Debbie's wide smiles, fears entertained within Victoria's pending appearance bringing disappointing news on making financial bargains good. Victoria, suddenly working girl's dearest friend, certainly resembled chief warrioress' positive aspects vis-à tackling concerns whenever decided.

Brassy attitudes conduced fearless business, envisioned entrepreneurs avoided dilly-dallying one bit, matters warranted serious dealings deserving proper conduct, faltering - wasn't at any rate condonable.

Before long, business completed, Miss Van Linden handed over two stuffed envelops anticipation compelled everyone's constant gaze on during newest *WG's* alighting earlier on, straight inside Debbie's eagerly awaiting possession, but first, moved pouch's flap aside, imperatively, circumstances required first ensuring presumed contents stacked up accordingly, moments later revealed contents.

Exposed pouch's constitution satisfied no one's expectations, indeed not, contents critically excepted dollar bills, Debbie espousing deep reservations about excluding banknotes amidst expected package handed over underneath dusky umbra, sounded convincing, tangible cash subsumed reasons Mrs. Charibert frowned upon everything, should lapses ever encourage disclosures little one indeed nestled close by Beacon Light's puzzle - looked inclined suffering great uneasiness, but ah! -good, good-tidings? -Victoria's impeccable logic tremendously sustained proprietress' lingering hopes. Contents instead comprised few bits, odds-as various ends personally satisfactory miss Van Linden's secondary associates heretofore unknown by chief warrioress handed over, knickknacks - many others--functioning covertly protecting any working girl's advantage whatsoever, but yearned linking identities, whilst hoping pledged sum helped see Beacon Light propositions succeed, Victoria's security grants wealthy Van Linden awarded tallied four or more thousand dollars - currently reposed within Chase's insured holding awaiting warrioresses-Victoria - finally enlisted incident upon tonight's rendezvous, later on, Debbie heeded constant self-advisement proscribing never again permitting simpleminded rewordings submitting remarks concerning wealthier folks.

As agreed upon previously during conversations, club's financier reiterated selfless efforts conserving club's purse stating continued wish guaranteeing occupying 'working girl's financial advisor status; coming across as one readily adapting personal efforts supplying clique most modern phones alongside desired novelties or surpluses success warranted, cash occupying top priority –for Vicky, everyone rested assured. Needless saying, Debbie jumped --as often recruitments warranted new incoming members earned work rig outs, thereafter, retraced steps towards family automobile patiently awaiting approach yards away on positions Victoria's strict instructions kept driver; Cuthbert Dilsomeworth adrift beside one female companion essentially constantly serving babysitters duties –shouldering delays.

As hurried steps carried club's financier past Livilda standing alongside Orelda Willoughby, waiting staff thrust carriage's doors wide open as Miss Willoughby articulated Victoria some fashion oriented catechisims,

"Excuse me ma'am, decked habiliments appear cotton, I presume-"

"Orelda--" retorted Victoria instantly, establishing outright recognition Orelda often craved-by vocal inflections heard countless times around Bessie Haynes, without visually verifying peculiar shadows lurking Mentone's darkness silently, "-dresses significances -or values associable with fabric used, pose minimal significance, we have work we must accomplish," -Victoria's chastising words encouraged quicker departures towards where Linden officially assigned enterprise automobile - awaited, soon afterwards departed Beacon Light - leaving little Debbie Charibert brimming widely. Several quick steps closed gaps till peers-slowly imbuing miss Victoria's remarks any possible accurate interpretations, impatiently awaiting whatever news rich girl brought along, stood abreast stood abreast themselves.

"All right girls," Debbie sounded assured, "all set, assayed work's all we visited here tonight-not merely spending time together –night's been good, I'm sure yours're worried stiff concerning your whereabouts, mine surely are, I not only presume, I know--"

"Mother's left town, father, too–" Livilda's response suitably comforted others,

"Mine are already asleep," Miss Willoughby informed Debbie, compounding Debbie's fear such infantile girls required harder work remaining club members much longer, however – regarding self, also reckoned much probabilities unwarranted absence must perturb Ayleth if discovered.

Evidently given impatience ostensibly written all over facial expressions, Mrs. Charibert seldom expected any delays outdoors during inopportune night hours whatsoever if groceries especially purchasing bean cans household intended consuming during supper, gave errand rise, except of course other necessities, or delays due Debbie's deliberate doing, situation increasingly warranted forming opinions of proper acceptable explanations usable in due course.

Small private chats between warrioress ensued briefly, but met intermittent interruptions Debbie posed gang. Thoroughly up against time, 23 Pecos beckoned expeditiously, Ayleth's patience no doubt runs out soon enough, besides, timeline allowed contained sparse minutes not beyond ten, no more, on countless occasions previously, Debbie accomplish similar errands within minutes spanning below five, tonight, five times five minutes–plus counting more - continued ticking: twenty-five no less après exiting. Young Miss Charibert certainly reckoned rightly on Ayleth's worries why on earth darkened outdoors continued keeping Debbie's bean cans away.   Summing evening activities up, Debbie supplied peers-seen equally bent on departure great advice,

"Desist confining all your eggs aboard one basket," warned Ayleth, agreements tallied concisely, interpretations consisting - ensuring shifting personal plans about, should spooks discover any one bit, others might yet remain obscure.

"How? -may I ask?" Orelda wanted every spoken word clarified, little Debbie explained as best possibly within Orelda's comprehension,

"I sincerely wish any willing new associates bent on giving Loving's project, well, suggesting all should also have individual minds set on alternate endeavors believed cast favorable pictures little girls growing up reputably appreciated," Orelda learned

All three girls parted ways soon afterwards, Victoria - left en-route towards family desperately simmering raucous proceeding due Helladius Van Linden's--alongside Victoria's mother's absence, party raucous progressed noisily –Orelda Willoughby's approached Hilltop Drive where transmissions on TV relayed best pictures during certain eras through an evening movies - Willoughby's never missed, even if supplied all known advancements deprived Loving, telecast presently on TV. Debbie finally darted off, Mickleburgh's stocked Hormel's holding several dollar notes mother provided, ready. Mrs. Charibert wanted several cans no more, or just two - if dollar amount earmarked bean cans sufficed, more if possible.

Fortunately, items not excluding refried beans Hormel's arranged fancifully on display shelves, many neared expiration dates-store owner wisely presumed warranted price reduction -'Mickleburgh instigated prices no less, amazingly, several dollars covered nearly four cans, but conveniently procured three.

Three cans satisfying most bean cans purchasable, little Debbie turned around departing Mickleburgh's premises barely collecting remaining nickels-whose counting disappointed covering another can, as usually quickened steps commenced ferrying delivery person nearer Mrs. Charibert.

Little Debbie's hurried step brought Ticehurst Cholmondeley's pub closer clutching two bean cans firmly, muffled voices - though failed hitting 'whisper' mark-whence uppity laden hubristic voices conversing made questionable utterances, but stood outside, utterances reaching forth, effected pronouncements implying–

"Admittedly, stated woman's strengths also perceived compassion, are very great," Debbie's hurried maneuverings slowed, facial parts containing curiosity keeled leftward onto Cholmondeley's low dimly lit window bathed dull yellow lights over outside where light beam fell. Stopping, two steps advanced Debbie one inch or two underneath wood braced sills, whereupon peeked over inside: one never knows possible discoverables, Debbie musted finding out undertakings affecting women - fold group's female companion felt qualified by, partying inside such dark roadside inns - highwaymen congregated once day's grueling activities ended, or umbra enveloped everywhere,

'*Peeking isn't triumph, Debbie,*' sensible self-admonishment dispensed internally, oafishness went without constituting personality, '*reason however exists on your side-Debbie,*' -obliged this particular cerebral voice typifying self-advisement, thereby sending itinerant little brat on tiptoes eight inches underneath Cholmondeley's obscurest windows, hoping observance respecting goings-on indoors, proved worthwhile,

"Oughtn't many contribute; Mm-?" Dr. Wakefield Debbie recognized much more easily wondered puffing hard on half burnt touted Cubans-none else certainly corroborated, others observed between tightly clamped lips, apparently, somewhat too inebriated, Mentone's singular physician; Hereward Wakefield-knowing more liquor suited constitution far less now, poised imbibing additional ounces.

"If ever success results, podiums are mine-I'll place-" another notable figure least expected gracing Cholmondeley's - given reputation, Mr. Van linden: oil mogul – bragged,

"Me too--" added store's kindly keeper, Aubourc, Shadowbrooks' too frequented Cholmondeley's, "I'll have congratulatory messages ready once all our wishes come true--"

"I'll have Cholmondeley's supply bean cans on opening day-" one, Debbie heard another barely audible voice referenced Sagard- though from Debbie's position, remained obscured by darkened hues surrounding Cholmondeley's interiors,

"Perturb thyself not-Sagard, I'll sing my heart out if ever our collective visions transpose onto reality--" -someone ponderously bean-cans laden eavesdropper outside-recognized as physician Wakefield vocal processes articulated.

Lowering gingerly onto roused heels one hurried moment occasioned antecedently by fleeing racketeers' presence, comfortable having some middle-aged woman subsisting alongside. Faint light beams thrown onto outsides through open windows on nearby houses abreast kept Debbie's little walking frame's sanity alive, one particularly revealed Chesserbottle further abreast 814 Pecos Street. Warrioress hastily-no doubts- headed towards Cholmondeley's-another notable Mentone sleazy hideaway hoodlums satisfactorily patronized ceaselessly during nights --but whose proprietor presently held exotic smokes between clenched lips inside Cholmondeley - although came across as very unlikely, Chesserbottle wouldn't spend sultry nickels more - unless necessary, price bill no cigar-save Cuban, veritably fulfills, permitting fraternizing amongst attending folks.

Debbie trotted on, making ideal connections each time resting households along Pecos- silhouetted by dusk, faded into Mentone's overhanging darkness behind, soon- Pecos street's most pertinent home still ways off loomed, beckoning. Instincts proved correct; on reaching Charibert's, occluding house's entrance - stood furious Mrs. Charibert barring Charibert bungalow's doorway - arms akimbo, routinely checking hour-minutes wristwatch indicated, then all over poorly lit streets ahead, impatiently awaited approaching young one's emergence any moment.

Reentrance beyond twenty-five minutes late occurred, Debbie knowing much about missing schedules - but on much less important matters, not father's bean meal nonetheless, observed inflections–one cross between grief's associative annoyances, convey Ayleth's misgivings,

"Debbie! -outdoor's been - ages, I can't remember last outdoors held your person outside this long?" -hinted Ayleth's maternal tones Debbie rightly apprehended circumventing further displeasures.

Transiently, several disturbing ideas crossed Debbie's mind- donning on extra one spare top dress brought along errand, one consisted spewing credible fabrications - how all interfering events caused unnecessary delays justifying longer stopovers Mickleburgh's often frowned on, or recount another untruth -how upon reaching Mickleburgh's promptly, found bean commodities demanded regular customer's constant patronage, already depleted, attending store environments looking about, awaited store owner's Hormel's bean can warehouse retrievals, or perhaps simply declare obfuscation by darkness, mistakenly detouring onto wrong routes, lost bearings due deep umbras surrounding everywhere, as such, having no flashlight guiding onward ways correctly, found steps proceeding oppositely, or perhaps just inform Mrs. Charibert, Chesserbottle's: errand's initial grocery store visited, required restocking Hormel's stockpiles, all supplies having sold out, thereupon felt overly compelled decided locating Cholmondeley's undeterred by Mentone's near pitch darkness, whereat encountered similar outcomes, eventually setting off Mickleburgh's way further down Pecos. But Debbie forbore uttering any such yadi-yadi-yadas, speaking untruths added up badly anyhow, little Debbie simply contended bravely–

"Pardon mother," yielded bean can messenger--dispensing sincere apologies, "working girls visited Beacon Light, I met one subsequently stopping by briefly, I wish I owned one smart phone –capturing one's glimpse could fetch us money-you know?" -unimpressed about Debbie's apology, Mrs. Charibert set aside immediate occupations inspecting one bean can's label, clarifying issues superseded everything else,

"I hope Debbie, friends hadn't compelled some goofing around– those ditsy schoolmates carrying big titles about, making waves?"

"Mother, I haven't," promised Debbie insofar as truths by half. Finally, Ayleth's mother-daughter mutual trust besides half-truths, malfunctioned, Debbie eventually breaking self-imposed rules forever sidestepping inaccurate facts mother passed on over this evening's Hormel bean cans, still and all, mother loved daughter dearly, daughter -on mother likewise. Assessing age-old ordinances of never feeding *'Mentone's best mother'*: -designation Debbie reserved Ayleth once absence, or farness encouraged confidence.

Debbie admitted herself back inside, convinced errand passed off appropriately after uttering substantively appeasing words Ayleth's hoped graced auditory perceptions during anticipated arguments, or conversation, should one choose describing interlocutions either-how, presently–

"I reckoned on taking errand easy, shopping worked out as anticipated, thereafter decided strolling leisurely as I could, tired feet needed rest --I'm sorry delaying supper mother, how about father? -Any signs father's back?" apologized Debbie one more time,

"Cheer up," accepted Mrs. Charibert, "Debbie, no such thing as delays betid Buchard tonight, two or three minutes remained till any worries are admissible dear, but I'm glad errand passed off successfully, do come inside" beckoned Ayleth already inside by two or four steps past Mrs. Charibert's position, "how many more cans have we?"

Gratified tempers leveled off once again, Debbie replied Ayleth,

"Three cans two dollar-twenty-eight cents mustered wholly, could've purchase one more on partial credit if any insistence, I believe broken cent changes covers one more purchase, here–three quarters change remaining."

Handing over: one, two, three quarter coins Mrs. Charibert quickly snatched, spinning around, sauntered back inside preparing continuing work on supper, followed closely by Debbie, each person thinking fascinating thoughts: whilst Mrs. Charibert wondered over making Charibert household most delectable bean meal Buchard ever chanced upon since marital onset presently spanning one decade-no less, conversely, little Debbie's dwelt on desperate measures Loving required if everyone's hometown must overcome ill fates many longed fixing - by helping Beacon Light shores sprout another New Loving –even more remarkably, anything but disappoint co-warrioresses whom immediate guesses included thoroughly enjoying reverence by folks wanting societal salvaging, none amongst working girls dared liken warrioresses' real situation akin flaming out.

Later on-during late evening, Chariberts' drowsily approached bedtime whilst mentally devising coming day's activities, Debbie's conclusions mirrored confidences-pending other matters, promising self - covert possibleness--much as societal paladins attained whilst numerous previous societal underhand affairs forged ahead, manage secrecy around New Loving.

Reaching over, two items: one notebook, then one lead pencil came off Debbie's bedside table whereupon quick journal entries covering today's activities entered posterity through literary works consequently awaited much scrutiny, latterly, flipped essay book's later pages as preparations reached actual jotting down coming day's plans prioritized itself, Mrs. Charibert's ignorance - young Debbie finally ranked alongside mobile people-owning amongst other luxury items, modern smart devices - all promise are as effective as any bought brand new, facilitating discreet calls close associates presumed likely, remained absolute, Debbie felt certain mother heard much small talk through grapevines - present avant-garde young females, find covert ways society handed over smart gizmos without parental approval, still could never suspect daughter Debbie equated such girls flaunting latest - well, not latest smart contrivances, except those as fortunate as Miss Van Linden, but ones good enough facilitating phone conversations, anywhere, anytime –anyhow.

Spent, Debbie slightly less valorous as convictions led on unyieldingly without fear, prepared sleeping, resolving keeping all obstructions away, assured herself handsome rewards awaited intrepidity.

LOVING COUNTY HEARINGS

Several mornings later, Debbie's school still being on vacation, Mrs. Charibert done visiting friends, returned home–chattering mightily over county's proposed court hearing days away wanting attendance, imploring Buchard's saving grace in providing absolvitory cover, any familial engagements scheduled during same hour as court hearings needed shelving to allow personal efforts impact county affairs during mornings; four, five or six days hence comprising all three consecutive days hosting proposed county courthouse inquests. Mr. Charibert's accession, brought two Charibert women great joys, Ayleth sought learning initiatives nursed by increasingly popular nonetheless obscure Beacon light girls, like Debbie felt youthful once more, but allowed minutest exhilaration, undoubtedly, variously aged females; girls, ladies, women, started out making waves once more - doing stuff, getting going-- if attending courthouses settling matters current affairs regurgitated, emerges as personal contributions, personal intentions subsumed canceling every reserved engagement however important, without question as per three day's hearings'.

Another two days passed, heralding day three assigned county court hearings' dawn, Ayleth Charibert departed early after casting aside thoughts Debbie's useful presence alongside trek, while 23 Pecos Street gladly hosted father daughter team's presence as each settled on tackling various assignments whilst mother visited associates.

Owing titbits Debbie grasped through continuous chatter endlessly engulfing Ayleth, suppositions hearings concerned edifices certain selfless young girls threatened erecting, overshadowed every transient thought: as variously stated through many precise descriptions detailing goings on, though, further commentary usually alluded 'promises' implicit within aforesaid 'goings-ons'; whenever easier day's work induced lighter mood about, as respects erecting residential tower blocks, Debbie learned no trifling matters entered debates, matters proposed hashed out dwelt primarily on young girls however ambitious, but also focused more on city planning, or on respecting zoning codes notwithstanding statuses actively involved contractors behind any proposed civil engineering projects cleverly fronted by young ladies, court also dealt masterfully on kabals populated by faceless men throwing weights around, later parts during sessions covered permits-related licenses one required as civil engineer whose occupation raises fine structures deserving places want --if noting eons old lakefront's designation as Mentone's most important recreational zones county satisfied fun-lovers cravings by conscientious county executives.

Even Debbie Charibert failed apprehending extents inherent meanings warrioresses' on going scheme affected society, unquestionably, working girls remained sole participants devising certifiable structures; edifices, estate, or complexes entailing Beacon Light's endeavor, non-subsequently, not even warrioresses served anyone smokescreen purposes, as diverse beliefs claimed severally, Debbie's cleverly surmised–whether rightly, or otherwise, that aforementioned county hearings touched Lego city directly, or if not, circuitously– Debbie suggested Livilda hear during an umpteenth conversation since acquiring handsets, how county protocol lacked authentic approach, no discernable parts composed previously assayed efforts on any records as being attempted discerning brains behind New Loving's rising. However, explanations interested Debbie's knowledge, hearings meant same as court cases anyhow irrespective titles authorities christened situation: hearing, appearances, adjudication, or court matter, someone exhaustively learned working girl's designs attempting hitherto unattained pursuits, immediately afterward instituted litigation.

Perhaps, Debbie during another lengthy clique members only phone communications, this time, Miss Van linden –accordingly surmised approaching matter no less paralleled county's official protocol, or actions undertaken by concerned county officials, one envious one, or perhaps - covert land grabbing actors - particularly Emmett Booth's Thornwood et al, hopes upstaging whatever orchestrations little girls harbored deep within young hearts, posted failures approximating caterpillar men's during initial encounter.

This explanation looked mostly true; neither Mentone nor Loving ever approached anyone known or suspected corroborated warrioresses' efforts remotely - allaying fears pertaining whatsoever-rumors bore concerning still unfamiliar little girls, intended installing.

Debbie's joys increased marginally, how warrioresses' skills remaining covert, saved everyone involved good griefs', being well aware - should participant's identities eventually suffer leakages as sandy Lego city--buildings nears braking ground or completing, every little scheme since thought through begins degenerating, or halts-none outside authorities' own circles courageously mustered challenges, nor showed minutest interests negotiating, maintaining crossed fingers, Debbie awaited hoping manageable news accompany Mrs. Charibert back - after day's court hearings.

Once instituted, bailiff's vocal chords stretching forcefully-carrying great sonances across, court session progressed slowly as usual, all sides embellishing mostly meaningless arguments as best possible, Emmett Booth's fellow Eardwulf Thornwood, rose up as Emmett stylishly brandished Longines' lavishly manufactured timepiece usually encircling one wrist whilst right arm tackled work, acknowledgingly, progressing legalities finally entered recognizable advance upon finish line with certain unapparent indices indicating favorable outcomes, Trimble's next remarks-indeed engendered hearing's fiercest eruptions through ensuing but needless arguments. Soon, today's hearings became passé, most barely withstood urges compelling immediately departing courtroom proceedings or environments, but still on cue after proceeding's dismissal,

Trimble granted defense counsel required authorizations, like everyone, hoped matter ended soon by ordering defense side's final interrogatories,

"If I'm correct, positions-as witnesses, continue being non awareness pertaining suspect's identities, some additional statements also hint on your places today as barristers representing plaintiff's interests, am I correct in my assumptions, mister–"

Emmett Booth sometime refuting Eardwulf Thornwood's remarks - fought over themselves, someone needed providing best suited responses, retorted simultaneously,

"I am," responded one,

"Oh-yes!" folks present heard Booth's fellow-Thornwood reply,

"State clearly –please, whose responses matter more? - yours? -stressed Aubourc making certain burly fellow-Thornwood received hints- "or mister–" -Aubourc said additionally indicating Booth, by way of response, caterpillar tag-team shot themselves recriminatory index fingers,

"Judge, should any confusion settle amidst prosecution counsels—" Aubourc hinted immediately requiring judicial intervention,

"Booth-" ordered Trimble, "I think, seem better put one between your prosecution duo," –no physical signs outwardly indicated such-however hard anyone peered, Thornwood's sweat induced fetors, or ones given rise by construction oriented toil, could never out stink Booth's,

"If someone–" -here indicating Trimble himself, "–insists," -agreed Booth flaunting wide smiles,

"Indeed, proceed therefore,"

Proper salutations almost convinced attentive court judge Trimble's great philosophical backgrounds, till–

"Your question?"

"As witnesses-like aforesaid, duties also incorporate as prosecuting counsels –right? -acknowledging Aubourc's reiterations, Caterpillar man duly surmised matter remained unresolved, under pertinent circumstances, issued next responses solely comprising-

"Yes, I am,"

"Then, say– list–as prosecutors, where working girls caused anyone around personal harm, prosecution team failed deciphered as witness?"

Uncertainties flickered on prosecution counsels' facial parts, leading Aubourc staging quick intervention attempts—for judicial procedure's integrity's sake, "I'll re-speak using more easier lingo, does vilifying young females barely beyond childhood ages sound appealing?"

Taken aback by case's best persuasive eloquence-yet Aubourc insightfully used delivering simple interrogatories, Booth, apparently not one very profound thinker, howled–

"Be silent!"

"Provide succincter responses Mr. Booth, no one has all day here--" admonishes Trimble somewhat abash over avoidable errors judging Booth's character, momentarily, everyone learned answers Trimble anticipated Booth provide, paraphrasing sermons preached on Beacon Light most recently, Booth enjoined court,

"Lawyers presume other folk's stupidities-others'll hanker after antagonizer's assistance once difficulties are imposed across one's way!"

None attending court successfully affixed accurate interpretations nor made head or tail within just voiced arguments.

Trimble's order dismissing matter later came as no surprise every relieved person inside county courtroom hadn't anticipated, excepting prejudicial dismissal, losing side'd dutifully rekindle diligences during next hearings argument'd start all over again.

Outside, further shedding light on Trimble's fallacious understandings, prosecution team threatened bystanders paying Aubourc heed, "Our powerful constituents demand all-out legal war, I promise."

"As are ours!" Aubourc's spontaneous answer reached back.

Recess ended all too soon, bringing warring parties back inside Trimble's courtroom, injunctions filed by land grabbers seeking influential ways on city officials-not excluding county executives or powerful Texas demagoguess, supplicating-please, help, please help, stop any unwanted onslaughts certain young unstoppables pose: new appellations no one ever applied working girls until prior mentioned court hearing moments ago, many certainties fell short on knowledge as respects exact Mentone parts, or families, or any surrounding towns around Loving marauding brats originated, projecting opinions: perhaps several - if not entire working girls resided elsewhere, but visited over, aiming starting unwarranted imperilments around peaceful localities none pursuing same causes shunned.

Court duly admitted further arguments, thereafter, proceedings progressed, one by one every person hired by litigious opposition gave testimonies why Beacon Light deserved pristine conditions enjoyed contemporarily. While portions frankly assumed waterfront's establishment resulted all those years ago due earlier Mentone folks desiring amusement parks county locals enjoyed, suggesting more covert, maybe openly endorsing additions opposition supported: elderly ones-county laws proscribed, reserved decision making rights over erections commencing yet or not, may perhaps carry, effectively instilling discomposure within opposition's side: defendants; any side settling court matters required presenting unified facts should side desire any guarantees, but right through onsets till presently, opposition presented disunited fronts, none being capable, nor managed establishing effective prosecutions perhaps plaintiff's hoped achieving - by instituting court matter: one side demanded Beacon Light's pristineness unscathed, while opponents hoped decision making authority allotted side-if any changes ever developed, judge Trimble however perplexed, took chances posing inquiries opposing attorneys ought present adversaries–how come naysayers presented disunited fronts, one legal terminology plaintiff's found so deeply confusing party fell over themselves researching old dirtied lexicons, judges inquiry prompted demanded clarifications concerning judge Trimble's 'disunited front'.

Trimble's immediate explanation convinced hearing's sizable audience, as county judicial officer spanning thirty-five years, never once encountered unprecedented events involving opposition handling legal issues presenting diverse representational units, one's argument favoring leaving situation without change, yet same prosecution unit making stringent arguments side ought decide outcomes or occurrences, presently unfolding inside county courtroom one, baffled all present, not least Trimble-given contents within an immediately publicized note once stringent scrutiny revealed legal documents contents side filed, no portions thereof indicated anyone or party, or parties named as defendants, judge demanded knowing if opposition frankly understood legal terminology: 'defendant'. Chief opposer duly informed judge Trimble affirmatives --concerning Emmet Booth, proper understanding ascribable 'defendant' lay within grasp, but immensely appreciates if Judge Trimble passed prosecution more clarifying explanation as regards alternative definitions any 'defendant' deserved handing county officials or courts irrespectively,

"By defendants," honorable Trimble explained, "I mean adversaries on your effort's receiving end—familiar side litigates against; folks, fellows, people, your diligences attempts stopping killjoys taking further nonapprovable actions, avoided raising any edifices wherever - inasmuch as your team constructs perceived buildings,"

"Oh, I see!" one opposition member none about cared hearing make utterances-following Trimble's persuasive explanation defining legal terminologies, alongside friends paranoid over court assembly recognized side as defendants if someone else first picked fights against cynical Mentone public by taking on building endeavors anywhere - effectively rendering anyone challenging as defendant, today's court visit occurred hurriedly,

"I see," came continuing replies, "defendants, ey?" -poor Hebblethwaite, visiting courts upon reckoning closed county records, showed uncommonness,

"Yes defendants, describe any known identities--" Judge Trimble demanded Hebblethwaite's clarification,

"Judge," began same Hebblethwaite fellow foolishly, "we miss out on certain required knowledge," Hebblethwaite explained, rearing an utterly filled courtroom B up laughing unrestrainedly, "all we know–" continued Hebblethwaite once laughter reentered manageable decibels, "–we intend stopping unapproved someone's erecting tall towers, our side must solely remain masterminds authorizing buildings –Ours! -Mentone typifies, do I get support folks?" Hebblethwaite's question particularly elicited grunts indicating agreement, thereafter no excitements matched Hebblethwaite versus Trimble exchange till session's ending.

First hearing passed, contentious matter locals all over Loving deemed 'hot potato', held onto everyone's attention not an ounce more than Debbie's fixated –often seen lingering around whenever Mrs. Charibert returned soon after hearings terminate; eavesdropping conversation between elder Chariberts served great purposes learning outcomes during proceedings during earlier day.

Tallying all information garnered by eavesdropping whilst courthouse events proceeded, Debbie made discoveries pertaining identities carefully wrapped up by certain litigants delightedly aspiring halting any profitable Beacon Light activities-warrioresses; girls plaintiffs never met, girls-none could recognize personally yet- heretofore barely possessed beyond blank knowledge about, yet embarked on litigation, none till now sunk complex building foundations on disputed soil, might someday reap benefits, no doubt, blank grounds couldn't signify construction blueprints, but– plaintiffs proceeded filing side's civil actions hoping courts bring whatever, or whomever lurked inside Loving County's shadows, deliberately refusing identifying herself or themselves publicly, untimely ends –Owing party's awareness actions side originated often generally repulsed Mentone's public: hence litigious action rests well under way.

Litigation sustained, court alongside everyone present succinctly assumed opposition's renegings concerning providing names identifying defendants pended afoot inside court's case, not least providing hearing dates, consequent upon unrealized judicial ordinances: named defendants unregistering appearances, hereinafter constituted judge Trimble's sole reason not dismissing matter that- entered court records titled: '*Naysayers .v. Warrioresses'* -hence, baffled everyone tremendously. Forthwith judge Trimble-much like everyone else, sincerely hoped opportunities enabling defendant's appearances soared, after all, matters strictly concerned Mentone, Loving County, or generally, one big Texas issue - actually deserving repetition --none reserved authorization augmenting structures in locations' laws already reserve as parks serving fun loving public warranted. Issuing directives characterized certain prerogatives as Mentone's onliest judicial officers of all similarly ranked persons, selflessly ensured opposing side's say some equality, presiding Judges atypically entered favorable judgments without opponents ever defending actions, as such, judge Trimble ordered further hearings commencing another twenty four hours hence verbalizing intentions as,

"I shall extend hearing another day or two," judge announced, "all parties've been very eloquent, court thanks the all."

"Cool, ha - ha" declared opposing side's head person still feigning innocence over attires admissible by court, detected thereupon-but as always clad raggedy denim overalls-bailiff-on judge's instructions, permitted during preceding hours.

Again, as discussion between Chariberts' over hearing's second day's transpirations progressed, Debbie sat mute feeling profoundly insecure, but cleverly pretending doing assigned schoolwork even though midterm vacation persisted, but literally stood still eavesdropping on discussions proceeding between parents.

"Still haven't discovered warrioresses' identities," declared Ayleth Charibert, directing county's most important sub-topics: certain girl's identities --still under discussion as regards Mentone's most pressing contemporary matters: presumed upcoming New Loving faceless individuals touted daughter age girls, no Mentone residents - not excluding any whatsoever, believed certainly contained any truths, but wished, as-such being true - signified womankind's maturity: however young, however old,

"Because–" -as one accompanying women visiting Charibert's during later evening–about 8 p.m, put matters-as discussions continued, "whomever makes up rank, if any such drive existed anywise, couldn't possibly equal young girls, young girls-I should think-" circuitously queried Ingrid Davenport: Wraxall Davenport's missus: Wraxall, sheep farmer proudly supplying endless meat commodities throughout surrounding lands, "-are busy underneath protective custody parents provide, none knows how authorities could ever suspect young girls harnessing unavailable resources erecting complexes, tall buildings, or new counties - like county government, perhaps state governments couldn't achieve– or whatever else epitomizes land grabbing Texan civil engineers, or executives, or County executives' credo?"

"Those constitute land grabbers conversations often addressed, everyone suspects maintains secretive involvement-supporting prosecutions against upcoming New Loving's proprietors," Buchard Charibert presented Ingrid Davenport's subtle suggestions-over which visiting lady's facial expressions sincerely displayed doubts, Debbie's father immediately added elucidative interpretations evening's small audience numbering two women plus--Mrs. Charibert, Ingrid, but also one accompanying less occupied man: Mr. Hewlett Cowlishaw, Wraxall's sibling upping tonight's outing, insisted on accompanying Mrs. Davenport hither Chariberts' abided, paying really keen attention. None felt predisposed betting bottom dimes unseen Debbie too- paid keen attention, all ears on unquestionably important topics.

On hearing's third day, Trimble ensured all side table forth discoverable briefs filed by anonymous individual, or individuals, took center stage - hinting clearly, litigation briefs insisted young daughter age girls master-minding grapevine oriented events-if accurate, reckoned illegal or unconstitutional making court appearances due incidental tenderness, making appearances due constant intimidation or reprisals Texas land grabbers - not least moguls dealing natural resources most certainly on standbys, threatened; if strangulations on anyone intent on usurping eminent domains, could help matters, such therefore sounded likely. Court's demands if site showed any ground-braking signs, directly addressing possible land grabbers: should current court session possess enough misfortune as gracing any such surreptitious presences,

How issues concerning 'involvements' fit questions warranting posing any aggrieved part resultingly allowing any further action on court's part enabling continuity, no one knows- courts however learned inceptive buildings foundations' stayed undetected anywhere around disputed Mentone vicinities, hinting also how figures responsible resolutely refused showing themselves:

one authentic response Judge Trimble's baffled court fell deeply silent spanning long moments. Instants after emerging induced silences, judge Trimble's court readied much awaited verdicts, judgments, decisions, even an order ensuring: 'aggrieved naysaying land grabbing party, opposition, embittered County executives, all reserved genuine cases considerable by any court, fell deathly silent as judgment neared disclosure -findings several chief hippies present-though muted, exclaimed unabashedly,

"Yeah!" -however, chief hippie: Evan Goldsborough fearing consequences should actions constitute court disruption, calmed down on realizations judgments inherent within Trimble's orders favored opposition whilst habitual riling occurred.

Soon after Goldsborough's epiphany judge Trimble announced opposition's inadequate proof any buildings neared construction near listed waterfront addresses - let alone break ground, following thorough scrutiny, authorities found no civil construction foundations indicated corresponding scenarios transpiring, or about; dissenting further, stated matters referencing building permits, zoning, licenses, rested solely underneath Mentone government's domains - not employees', or sympathizers –whatever persisted anywhere, however heartfelt, or -wrenching, shouldn't pass muster as personal issues individuals deem combatable on whims -on additional contentions, opined-concerned individuals tagging alongside prosecution, incompetency providing court one defendant, or list thereof assigned answering interrogatories, stating how finally given contents within document's foregoing's: astounding failure identifying distinguishable defendants, also opposition's shortcomings serving named defendant, or -s -whomever fit descriptions therein, documented court briefs required if matter must progress judiciously. Court's injunction utterly oblivious considerable other choices remained, championed entirely by enraged Trimble, through squeaking halts, prematurely terminated yet another frivolous matter, thereupon advised plaintiff's-presiding judge cared not aggrandizing through identifications, judicial reasons ensuring person's named adversary-aggrieved side hopes occupies legal battle's short ends next time, are duly served appropriately dated court papers instructing appearance on any day court hearings holds.

At any rate-circumstances seemed, Debbie's warrioresses enjoyed safetics obscurities provided still, land grabbers, executives besides being crooked tycoons hiddenly instigating opposition activities posted misadventures given this first instance assaying halting warrioresses' onslaught.

'Single penny's given one's thoughts', following judicial outcomes, Debbie feeling incalculably emboldened since big encumbrances as opposition, couldn't cause anymore impediments, let alone small ones as thoughts or beliefs powerful minds toted about, or assayed recently, though failed, faltering rather badly –as mother often reflected during diverse matters, actions, comparing words, spoke louder each time, words-no warrioress forbade uttering, yet, failure abounded naysayers, watched by all existing Loving county–but without perception, 'concerning personal positions, efforts already began proving substantiality about Mentone's redevelopment, thereafter keep Texan court- or authorities thereof's matters pending, just wait- folks!' --gloated little Debbie whilst personal waiting endured–

FINAL PREPARATIONS

    *V*ictory secured, nowhere else besides increasingly plentiful little girls' land grabbers threats embodying preventive measures against further development if not bought over, perhaps bribed, or apportioned out any available county pudding: Debbie swore long ago never allowing, appropriately engaged joyous moods; Debbie hereinafter, endeavored capturing two birds on one stone's throw.

    Increased activities on smart phones acquiesced constant communications between warrioresses, one often calling another on flimsiest grounds - as pasta strands continually falling off fork prongs, or– how cortina's size seven comparatively fit feet tighter where 'loafers' size six wobbled.

    During one lengthy chitchat till odd hours arrived, Victoria finally accepted fully-fledged warrioress amongst peers, thereafter, regular conversation incorporating old timer-Livilda's opinions increased marginally, establishing convictions Debbie's likelihood abandoning old alliances if newer ones came along, were minuscule. As aforesaid, lengthy conversations seemingly never ceasing, unnecessarily ensued mostly -nevertheless, no topic underneath heaven - likely aged girls thought intriguing enough inherent elements warranted centering conversations, escaped treatment-whether or not proper sensibilities derived. Despite all contributory significances–disregarding source, or lack thereof, mere minute information insomuch as common knowledge-eavesdroppers working government agencies whilst applying specialty electronic equipment along with select catch phrases, or industry standard terminologies, often intercepted private chats, occasionally detecting young girls vocally hashing out serious matters, ever found traces leading authorities towards culprits, thereafter, commenced investigations - not on questions whether parents' authorization permitted ownerships, but why; Beacon Light, lake front, waterfront et cetera, featured prominently all through records of particularly wiretapped conversations, accordingly, warrioresses busied themselves learning coded quatrains, cleverly misrepresenting terminologies indicating circumstance all involved certainly felt might potentially disclose important clandestine activities nosy fellows eavesdropping detailed conversations sought after, but without absolute comprehension attributable 'bugged' discussions --Notwithstanding if encryption worked, preventing interference by authorities, warrioresss went without sufficient knowledge-or none by any chance, but each morning, during still enduring vacation, saw Debbie cleverly avoiding Ayleth, once chores finished --sometimes exigently, heartbeats further on, reentered private quarters-hurriedly resuming conversation any working girl manning opposite ends set up by calling, thereafter, begin exchanging ideas.

One particular phone conversation ideally provided warrioresses delightsome opportunity reaching agreements on possible means amassing facilitative equipment detailed construction work ahead inclined toward repining.

"Dear-" Livilda's father inquired hoping Albree-Mrs. Ravenshield's earlier good moods persisted, time showed barely twenty-four hours after Mentone's historical *Naysayers .v. Working girls* litigation reached much deserved termination everyone prayed judge impose, "I stowed shovels inside attic closet two, has anyone seen any shovels around? -attic's usually shovel storage," -Albree Ravenshield briefly depicted one lodged behind attic's doors months ago, not past several days, Mr. Hereward loading shovels inside attics as claimed failed cluttering Albree's memories like earlier events ineligible one bother inserting inside Debbie's narrative, after all, individual activities never compelled one's usage, thenceforward, 'issues-arising' missing shovels engendered inside Ravenshield household, passed quietly once Hereward suddenly became uncertain one ever stayed here.

Come morrow's morning--

"Arthur, Arthur-" inquiries Albree Ravenshield directed Livilda's younger sibling's circulated: Arthur's auditory perception, demanding Hereward's pickaxe's whereabouts caused Arthur slight chills --presently, item sought no longer met descriptions as same shovel Albree sought last time whilst utensil deposited behind store room doors, Ravenshield often employed-tearing-felled tree stumps apart around residential front yards whenever warranted, Arthur, sometime branded Dave, like Albree, denied ever knowing whence household's pick axes rested.

Next, one day prior Debbie's unwavering resolution on breaking ground on vicinities county judge instituted moratoriums, warrioresses commenced much awaited work - by first creating fun-all around atmosphere: young misses' own strategy preventing precipitating actions inviting guilty judgments following possible uninvited intrusions --otherwise face charges relatively involving child abuse-consequent on interfering with minors subjecting selves through construction work constituting part thereof learning process --much as could be brought against intruders attempting interferences, plus indictments furthering 'harassing minors' too.

Victoria's industrialist father, Helladius Van Linden, laboriously howled vocal chords hoarse, why anyone removed treasured cement bags put away inside storage rooms, complaining loudly personal records showed six stockpiled, not five, but six bags containing cementing substance aiding proposed fossil fuel rig's construction untapped oilfields along vast Texas coastlines must give up, Van Linden however made certainties known,

"No father-" -riposted Thruppy Van Linden, but could have been Manton, Victoria refused disclosures during narratives passed Debbie; Thruppy likewise Manton being dependable younger siblings --whosever's were uttered denials. However, guilt missing cement bag prank now being discussed, vented all around, rested squarely on either boy's shoulders --but gone anyhow fifty kilogram worth of limestone was. Similarly, across all twelve houses across Mentone, like many populating surrounding towns; plenty utensils, tools, amenities, equipment-family members discovered missing–household nevermore found, resultantly- might have been presumed lost, stolen or inappropriately removed should owners crave usage, but fell short establishing legitimate Beacon Light connections, nor could missing items be explained due Debbie's unusually prolonged absences Ayleth scarcely adjudged correctly after countless guesses.

Donations– girl's club direly needed some, many-somehow turned up in truckloads; structure molds donors supposed some usefulness; auxiliary knickknacks construction often required- individuals purchased, others borrowed, others lent, countless many made donations - all-reached warrioresses' designated storage points on timely basis –Little by little, time approached New Loving's main towers construction.

During later evening yielding groundbreaking morning, Debbie Charibert located household's oddments stashed away somewhere; shovels, pans, scoops, twines, containers, more cement bags, tape measures, every bit illegally associates' families, or unfamiliar people befriending Debbie's associates, found missing, Victoria fared well circulating word, using widely established associations, amassed much donations, thereby depositing process on irreversible paths, retracing steps now - all agreed, unfathomably countered groups mantra, Mentone events promised supervening all preexisting undertakings irrespective of muscles executive everyone's vis-à officials, put up as challenge, or attempts stopping progress.

Ground breaking gathering completed as expected: warrioresses' recruits: unconnected school children resolutely sworn never divulging information whether fathers-as mothers made demands, reluctant siblings-too - even one bit, stood attentive - eagerly awaiting work each envisaged authority emanating, main pictures situation illustrated Debbie consisted one showing– 'all hands-being on deck'. Through hours heralding dusk, Devil-advocating, Debbie's desperation soared reaching high heavens, all alone, visited work sites during inopportune hours anticipating none else's hand or hands' making up accompaniments on deck alongside. Inasmuch as such inopportune hour warranted company, Debbie Charibert lost countless instances finding warrioress willing night time ventures: sneaking through bedroom windows, typically descending fifteen foot ladders yielded downwards by top floors girls' rooms-like Debbie's often occupied in most homes, downwards on grounds below, working girls expected great rewards steadfastly helping erect brand new counties - championed by one associate; Debbie Charibert, still– every last one swore oaths protecting secrecy–not risking lives, or limbs –consequently, made solemn promises sneaking out should henceforth prioritize lending as many hands building New Loving --although hinted, such efforts should never include sneaking downstairs through windows unseen eyes remotely viewed as procedural part, risking limbs, or life periodically: much hogwash circulated recently, more still circulating: how girls, boys also, stuck out stealthily through many home's front obscured by night, or through back doors, through attic windows, upbeat about leaping downwards, but most surpassingly, through telescoping ladders placed on walls beside closest windows, tripped, breaking limbs trying, none wished augmenting available statistics, but introduced Debbie all necessary promises one required gingering onward.

Every cloud boasts silver lining came multiple self-consolations once wisdom, or plurals therein, disclosed kind words as mere promises cleverly egging all-not only Debbie on during this later stages, after all, peculiar positions deviated not too far aside all historic women's exertions sowing overarching differences, though, activities championed by women throughout recent years witnessed depreciating intensities, nevertheless, here exists Debbie Charibert taking over leadership batons history's most enterprising women remembered once championing causes worth remembering.

DON M DENN

Feeling blue recently, minor ailments though –since proper hourly functioning; taking time out moving around, thinking clearly, bodily temperatures being well within acceptable standards, continued, therefore suspected physical slow-downs heavily weighing anticipations roused, diverse overwhelming matters not hitherto anticipated, often caused further melancholy; once hunkered down, most people placed trust on grapevines - Debbie Knew

Like most females, chief warrioress detested feminizing 'hero - into 'heroine' –preferences tacked more onto masculinity: insisting appellation:- '*hero*' certainly augmented reputations within thoughts, individual acclaims nevermore retained not outside grapevines, since reputation thereafter permeates talk all over towns maybe beyond, as great hero, or maybe better put - heroine, not Mentone's, or Loving's, but Texas - or beyond.

Struggling onto bed Sunday night-occasioning Monday morning Debbie billed construction's commencements, mesmeric thoughts of 'how on earth hitting good marks attempting burrowing underground by recruiting more like Warrioress-Victoria, accompanied by many faceless those Victoria brought along covertly without declaration, majorly constituted on goings, much hope rested on Victoria Van Linden's assistance: peerage thought-definitely resulted due momentary spurs: jumping on band wagons, wanted roles allocated them as any progressing good ensues, perhaps anything under any circumstances, promised more, previous ones thitherto mostly kept, then purposefully managed keeping preventing failure –well, success oriented mingling, takes tow - one assumes -if correctly, warrioress'd overheard Buchard Charibert advising Ayleth's on occasions winding down during certain evenings, one wise saying Debbie thought perfectly suited this all-encompassing situation provoked by Vicky Van Linden - petroleum mercantile's own, willingly forking over large sums enabling Vicky's- as Mr. Van Linden fondly reserved –best wishes everyone hoped associate-Debbie's ultra-modern New Loving erection, truly manifests.

PHOENIX RISING

    Debbie's utterances vis-à: tango taking two –perspectively viewing Victoria's promises, made manifest on construction day -five days prior vacation's end, little did everyone's heroine: hero-whichever suited one's personal preferences-as little Debbie Charibert's appellative aliases --know Miss Van Linden's instructions given sibling: Manton Van Linden, carried across perfectly; Manton made certain every long associative fellow promptly assembled Beacon Light awaiting dignitaries on named morning-wall oriented calendars coincidentally showed fell within Debbie's free day: Tuesdays-elder Chariberts' seldom paid any meaningful attention, leaving young female ward attending each one's own devise privately inside Charibert's Sprawling bungalow, or anywhere Charibert yard accommodated presences, doing whatever fancifully dominated imaginations.

    During earlier months, Ayleth's curiously noted daughter Debbie' Tuesday habits, young one spent all hours singing, sometimes joyfully drying laundered clothing on low lying lines behind Charibert's bungalow attached wherein one could simply climb whereupon sit on any suitable branches, whilst whiling away time. This one preoccupation annoyed Buchard Charibert somewhat, as enfeebled tree branches do give way, permitting great falls then severe injuries. But on this Tuesday, laundry excluded festoons on lines alongside frolicking Debbie --on today's occasion, Mrs. Charibert missed hearing any overbearingly sweet voices-singing songs carried nigh by Mentone's uneasy breezes, on Buchard's part, none perceived worries over viewing someone 'much revered' hanging on tree branches-though clamoring branches often remained patient awaiting approach, on this Tuesday, Debbie ensured Ayleth received warnings about impending outing-visiting waterfront whereupon ascertain if any intruders approached Beacon Light,

    "Indeed-" agreed Ayleth, "pleasant idea I presume, please do let us all know those silly girls designs,"

Had Mrs. Charibert initiated moves preventing young one's exiting today, Tuesdays being days Debbie often owned all alone, prohibition could potentially have become situation's proverbial last straw…, but little Debbie Charibert tactically finessed ways around situations, today– free Tuesday-no less, one day's sufficient allowances as deemed fit until early evenings or thereabouts, as an effect, requesting visitation permission covering elsewhere: library, Mentone museum-if one still functioned, or even Lakefront successfully visited countless times previously upon obtaining visitation permits granting temporal absence, chances were, granting little one such privileges mattered -given proper considerations, fittingly sought permission Mrs. Charibert duly granted moments later. Ayleth's denial -insofar as Debbie surmised, could potentiate first ever occasions unapproved construction activity commenced without leading personnel, proper work etiquette considered, collective travails usually took off upon leader's appearance, Debbie being sole instigator, little else, or person mustering all probabilities of effectively kick starting drives, not Livilda, not Victoria - irrespective of being quite capable of directing group's affairs - half as good, nor providence, nor chance; just one known person could erect New Loving solely applying wits alongside bare knuckles. Considering herself– Loving's own, that despite everything, Loving stood built.

These thoughts constituted beliefs as Little Debbie Charibert sauntered daintily onto Charibert household's outsides, wherein open streets slightly breezy atmospheres expressed turbulent greetings along with several passing locals, pacing harder, increased footsteps enhanced hopes of arriving waterfront not one minute past eight o'clock dot, ensued.

Beacon Light roved over half mile away, Debbie long acquired skills tracing several routes entering hallowed grounds-whether or not blind-folded. One particularly veering leftwards - compelled greater feature's recognition without second thought after constant previous usage. Wheat street meandered right through town arriving county's vantage point, but upon several times recently - during wandering along afore-indicated leftward route, familiar folks briefly stopped, questioning destination or inquiring parents' whereabouts, subsequently took alternative roads scarcely containing any crookednesses, or any low hills, notably presented longer yet more pleasant passage allowing attendance wherever without elders interfering.

Assuring herself trekking situation warranted cleverly finessing around obstacles: long often scanty expanses, few portholes dotting evenly paved roads, also dotted this rightward road's expanse, Anderson Ranch Road often quickly saw Debbie safely back home. Debbie's advent eventuated as men undertook working, suitably placing pre-manufactured house molds where needed. Victoria -one last most active associate resolute on tackling meaningful travails since arrived, soon afterwards, commenced hearty chitchats, containing comforting information chief warrioress's expressions beseeching, requesting Victoria enlist associates anywhere influences extended - hopefully-Texas - Van Linden's frequented often --thereat obtain friends' pledges, was met.

Transiently, miss Charibert detested Victoria's charisma masterfully kick-starting work without first obtaining leader's permission or knowledge, as afore stated, New Loving being Debbie's baby merited nobody else declaring plows commenced, not Miss Van Linden's. Filled with apprehension, each little step furthered Debbie closer, thereupon observed work site already harbored inured population comprising Vicky alongside twenty-five odd studiously jobbing boys, no doubt pupils Loving's two or three main elementary schools produced, cleverer judgment aptly suited conclusions inherent within 'letting sleeping dogs lie', whether or not Victoria commenced kicked off work, mattered little, rebuilding New Loving originated nowhere else but within, an idea originally personal, Victoria - however sweetly disposed, however rich- appropriating much efforts supporting hitherto unconnected projects, hadn't Miss Van Linden - hereinunder listed as employee number six whilst signing signatures issuing large finances Debbie's project implicitly desired, distinctly established hierarchy between Victoria Van Linden's duties when comparing chief executive official's - overseeing operations, thereafter, Victoria's position as foreman could energize labor erecting edifices, but--on Debbie's order -but as an assistant.

Foregoing explanations seemed satisfying, still- preferred serving ground breaking day as voice issuing commands working men must heed upon construction tasks raising New Loving.

Bundling little pleasure puffs up, Debbie-on arriving work zones realized construction only neared entering commencement stages, huge smiles fifty four witnessing eyes spied register on Debbie's face, let more bagged cats out, chief warrioress lacked proper sensibilities excusing supervisory omissions mandatorily inscribed on many contractual documents, nor possessed expedient behaviors on seeing boys working New Loving project on another's behest, Victoria- too– detested apprehending hear-says personal contributions warranted due Debbie's 'raised' objections or authorization –cutting short any tattletales. Soon after duly shaking twenty workingmen's hands - figuring out how such familiarizations reached every Mentone's elementary school, perhaps beyond-but which Debbie refrained asking, each working girl simply set up task on-Debbie's instructions.

Morning's numerous prospects progressed, work everyone noted–too- picked up steam, Debbie waited but upon realization pundits:- anyone willfully pinpointing questionable motives lurking behind advancing project, instead, many poised uttering argufying syllables, wanting-by personal utterances - teach placing molds more expertly, or how expertly guided sand pours erecting New Loving's mansions, offices-as buildings accessories wherever Debbie wished aesthetics around historic second Phoenix rising venture finally nearing earnest commencements enhanced - comes about, raised voices all around barking out orders hoped carried out as instructed-if work must proceed smoothly - as each boy dug up more dirt, hoping personal efforts out-drudged others' if minding Debbie's instructions: Debbie's own ingenious little way effecting methodical madness pursuing agendas hampered by various obstructive activities –none about uttered convincing verbosities insinuating caution, or one attempting discontinuing process undeterred by imposingly grandiose terra firma bound blueprints filling out workman's visions on spots holding each boy hostage, contributing selflessly summed up optionally as astute help completing tasks accordingly, till this point-all hands originally but erroneously envisaged being hers alone, fortunately, presently counted lots numbering beyond all anticipations initially, labored, as soon, Victoria's phone tinkle arrived Debbie's Motorola during one specific moment supervisory styling–overseeing laboring men work hard, continued.

These typified workmen, workmen-not without much sparkling decencies, nor styled as ones playing without fully functional brains or intellect, verily, artisans checked out smart, properly playing around situations if any ever hoped earning either's senior warrioresses' tight hugs - feasibly-kisses; supposing any stood real chances deriving beneficial impulses one's great wits dictated -or miss Van Linden's plentiful life's frills everyone else desires. Pictures do really paint thousands more last impressions beyond words ever could-as alliance men labored on tirelessly, genuinely reminding Debbie fortunes betid-helming unique happenchances occurring once during five, perhaps four, four cumulative lifetimes--no one knows, but however awe inspiring anyone attributes current visuals– hired hands toiled-exerting great sinews, establishing working-girl's collective's labor as mere- 'walk inside Debbie's Park'.

Thank goodness, Debbie-by similar tokens as Victoria's, accorded assent, propounded ideas seemed workable; first settling significant issues covering: leadership, superintendence. Debbie might have considered pulling wool over associates eyes: in re– wool over Victoria's perfect vision - harnessing vain glorious boasting skills Debbie learned over time, conversely, Victoria: over hers utilizing empty promises, after all, Debbie–as with Victoria, enjoyed swell poll positions retractive through onsets.

Delighted onto pride, as little Debbie Charibert's workmen, twenty odd boy's –soon becoming –as spontaneous self-christening defined, *'secret boy alliance assisting Loving's good'*, toiled away, often admonishing individual incapacities exerting even more work oomph over attempts-all increasingly observed ebbed downwards till equating child's play, none amongst peers essentially elected one's presence here as mere witness or observer, inclusion entirely thithered around contributions –leaving proprietress astonished over alliance boys' sources acquiring prerequisites enabling such arduous tasks, '...*never mind*,' many toiling hard workers paraphrased self-advisements maintained, much strife usually helped much later once hitting sacks during bedtime,' during hours most folk's insomnia lasted during each passing night, managing lingering thoughts dwelling on either enterprising girls overseeing work, knew much pronouncement. One hitherto reluctant young Mentone local boy: Drogo, Mr. Wolstenholme; disheveled shaggy haired child, arrived late, presented school identifications, thereafter received New Loving's real estate job spot, afterward reentered drudgery modes - working harder.

Work- shrouded by judge Trimble's order preventing authorities' further interruptive inquiries or obstructing Loving's redevelopment - continued without cease.

Following news numerous supplication by interested locals during one particular passim telephone interlocutions Debbie engaged secretly simultaneously telephoning Victoria besides Livilda, lest Mrs. Charibert discover daughter's unauthorized smart phone possession, humoring supplications requesting New Loving inhabitation.

Later on whilst discussions progressed as dusk enveloped Mentone, Debbie's also learned - one or two gas baron's concerns about questionable activities beleaguered lobbyists induced - as all similar ventures intricately involved profitable schemes accomplices could obtain discommensurate profits, hence more robbing satisfaction many potential rivals portending patronage pined achieving, or supporting upcoming county under pioneership by local daughters vis-à lakefront's redevelopment, thus- correctly entertained cheerful dispositions brought on by this news about town: each wished contributing determinations bent upon making times more tolerable –unreservedly agreed.

Part of news circulating touched back on earlier incidents six years ago, when-- days after Buchard Charibert bequested Debbie Lego City Adrastus & Sons-General stores, Inc, Austin, Texas, sold, instructing permanent keep where installed just beyond cradle's headboard, elaborately built toy buildings, Buchard thought, could help dear daughter apprehend more about big city life during growing up years, then aspiring somewhere else could be home. Five-year-old afterwards entertained massive epiphanies: *installing graven effigies of every Mentonian sufficiently solved age-old issue of preventing locals emigrating further afield seeking lands unknown,* five-year-old Charibert daughter traversed around Charibert bungalow on Pecos' interiors - dogged by thought bubble hanging overhead, reckoning-- locals submitting effigies of themselves folk's child's housing authority'd apportion living accommodations inside reserved tower models was all required if Mentone wished keeping each last person native without ever conjuring big cities dreamily–let alone approach one, amid momentary spurs, sent locals-sometime multiple invitations requesting everyone surrender effigies by mail addressed: 23 Pecos Street, or Bessie Haynes Elementary school, pending placements inside aforementioned pinioned Lego City alongside another much larger one proposed built somewhere though indeterminate Mentone much later.

Fearing abandonment following resurfacing of six year old determinations, stories circulating grapevines compelled judicious self-advisement on many Mentone's newer forward thinkers, each approved situating little graven selves each person's visual acuity confirmed exact likeness of one inside vacant Bessie Haynes elementary school classrooms designated-'*collection points*' manned by one warrioress posterity later recognized as none other, during hand over events tagged: 'second phase' transfers - strictly speaking, of effigies, upon these returns– sought augmenting tally of folks eagerly awaiting modern abodes, symbolizing actual home's binary matching - provided each interested local, as Loving continues investigating ways internal strife could quench earliest thirsts Mentone, or Loving County since nurtured wanting elevated ranking amongst higher Texan societies --as proper domiciliary structures quite capably forestalls later cravings –until one attains advancement.

Interested parties burgeoned marginally, first responders trailed back home where certain Mentone vicinities beckoned - often on reconnaissance seeking out good accommodations, many lingered, enjoying phoenix rising's immediate scenery, disparate several swaggered around recognizing each's counted blessing as pivoting around each building walked past-keeping great distances from work site - as fantasies imagining better days intensifies, rising higher, nosing upwards facing horizons merging onto often fabled silver linings lining skies beyond.

Copious requests numerous locals making up almost everyone staking out 'New Loving' residences, Debbie regularly communicated others, reached existent mayor's homework table just beside pinioned Lego city east end, but first, ensured each applicant's unique contributions aided progressing redevelopment, subsequently, continued disallowing naysayers any swagger anywhere near New Loving, as most putatively supposed no favorable permits hung unresearched on owner's desks, hoping matters continued similarly. Pensive, Little Debbie dispatched promisory notes containing accedences through subordinate peers: folk's accommodation requests seriously affected issues around office, perforce must meet immediate resolution, unauthorized swaggering's - whether–tranquil or otherwise about town by those assured places augmented preventable worries sheriff's office abhorred, if only privately - lest senior Charibert come under indictment as 'kill-joy'.

Informing folks convenient requisites on several conditions Victoria's trustworthy suggestions derived; stipulated charitable transaction must intrinsically incorporate, or leastwise well-wisher's best wishes, good prayers-everyone acknowledgedly needed, orderly conduct filing out proper housing papers, else- assume corporeal involvements within brick by brick edifices' erection, or, perhaps diplomacy- if exclusive offer of serving sorority any good purposes as project's solicitor, accordingly satisfies warrioresses as well orientated, assigned duties sanctioned handsome rewards determinable by everyone's truly, or by contributed tokens.

However, established protocols-instituted by itinerant young female entrepreneur, encouraging natural gladiatorial outlooks irrefutably observed forsooth against powerful land grabbers supported by corrupt paper weight political forces facing continuing battles encompassing Loving, or as many believe, fast approaches occurrence, but must first enter quiescence empowering Victoria's successful supplicants; themselves– friends, families, alongside few notable allies, may prospectively attain good assignable residences, or club houses, or any purpose whatsoever warrioresses' harmony indicated needn't exclude others save financial establishments, meetings earned approvals, guaranteeing any transactions under such circumstances-nonetheless felt much honored thanks due mounting requests obligatorily received frequently.

ABANDONED UNTAPPED BEAUTY

*E*xhaustive work by toiling men progressed earnestly underneath Mentone's cloudy skies, working-men numbering twenty or thereabouts: each feared relenting lest such individual become 'working chains weakest link' -work therefore continued gradually, layering more atop another layer, mounting pithy handfuls by pithy handful, abandoned beauty, Phoenix, as legends suggested, rose steadily, soaring skywards little by little.

County court judge Trimble's order-Debbie, Livilda Victoria absolutely perceived as possessing every known divine hallmarks preventing uninvited guests approaching proposed building site beforehand, or instituting suppressive activities over whatever construction work entailed, did much good-besides whomever footed associated bills, held, orders sustained irrevocably. Somewhere nearer 3 p.m. than not, working men spied little warrioresses dancing quick beating hearts out while workers toiled on,

"Very well apprehended," several submitted consolations voiced by young John Shakerley seen toiling harder moments after speaking alliances opinions as holding hands together, warrioressess' joyous dance continued, "we," Shakerley stated bowed busy repositioning already set molds, "every boy fancies dating either soon--"

"One'd teach wisdom, another'll ensure we have all nice stuffs our fantasies hints upon constantly,"-affirmed James Shuttleworth - thereafter, determined one particular structure assigned none other's energetic application needed readjustments, James Shuttleworth set commenced jobbing.

As dusk descended over everywhere gradually obscuring still grooving girls, questions whirled around twenty-two noggins, Victoria's own questions centered on how soon actual buildings Debbie's vision induced hard workers onto giving construction every effort making, becomes possible—Debbie's perspective however being; how long, or how much efforts pending labor gets houses populating everywhere?

Without doubt, about twenty sworn hard workers remained behind tackling more drudgery, ceaselessly doing enterprising warrioresses - most notably Debbie's-biddings -comrade having acquired stomach bug infection, resultingly dropping out sniffling, consequently suggested urgently visiting nearby infirmaries emergency rooms, as working men's complaints reached excited dancers' ears: one obtusely large Chrysler automobile Helladius Van Linden's Oils owned, arriving party comprised workers minded such duties as ferrying Victoria about coming - intending ferrying stricken alliance's workingman away. Several boys gazed on-by visual acuities, established retiring patient as chubby Thruppy Linden, Victoria's other sibling famously known omitting family's middle initial 'Van', concerning goings-on central character's reflections over identities occupants ultimately bestowed beautiful edifice's - working men erected one after one more --How much Mentone population warranted constructing beautiful canopies numbering thousands? –easily satisfying housing needs every Mentone family ever pondered multiple times over–

As girlish jollities progressed, abstractions lingered; all available record show about forty-five families-perhaps less settled Mentone - raising general population not beyond three hundred; right after clocking two hours-or slightly more after constructions commenced, twice more homes equating general populations, stood erect, later on, during closing hours-ending construction's first day, seven being ones constituting total construction periods earmarked, parts inherent within oration little Debbie delivered workingmen an hour after arrival-whereupon met each awaiting patiently, spewed forth encouragement but soon after halted construction following decisions all twenty remaining laborers during second hour mark required inspection, each needed-thus ergo– awaited information riddled disquisitions. Debbie ceremoniously introduced herself as Little Debbie Charibert: sole New Loving's proprietor, therefore payroll master belatedly administering working men's salaries, assertively informed all-following two hours jobbing, alliance workmen somehow finally managed usurping land grabber's roaring thunders –rivals, not excluding corrupt executives everyone happily noted during subsequent chats - excluded every participating working girl's parents, hence continuing Beacon Light presences --competition, continued amidst County executives polls -time after time revealed comprised mainly unspecified parent's willful support, much as Buchard Charibert's.

Each boy's jubilation following Debbie's announcement keeled rather heavily onto exuberance - though not one shown upon finally meeting esteemed Little Debbie personally, nor handful's perceived standpoints time kids took necessary action needlessly challenging status quo.

Hindsight thrust into perspective three days hence-earlier today considering Debbie's calculations, realized appreciable fallacies taking working men's jubilation negligibly, Debbie feared widespread exhaustion few hours after commencement, inciting discontinuations, touting how everyone's expended possible best's, thereafter request allowance retreating homewards, initially slowed headway–crush on working girls, or no --but here labored all, three days hence, exerting individual drudgeries as ones setting out on tasks augmenting cumulative efforts successfully manifesting more erected towers-surpassing entire Loving's population. Everyone, familial pets too, could without pointless ado, if desirations pressed, own several homes apiece.

"Whose are these? –towers efforts shall raise, Debbie Charibert?" -corresponded great nagging questions circulating thoughtfully within Debbie's mind, heart, or head -none knew still –wearied locals increasingly fled where greater Texas provided more civilization following indications of such's absence within Mentone notoriously bereft such features as; nightlife, social gatherings anywhere, never consisted beyond one dozen, plus– currently toiling working men, one solitary account historical tattle tale claimed involved social partying occurred during 1800's right after Loving: Oliver-mister, rose into limelight claiming Loving county's birth till date, remained sans any memorable runanga's, except nineteen young Lovingers, Mentonian's perhaps, plus several exiting elsewhere enroute hither, gathered, honoring secret phone calls between warrioresses once early evenings came around each day, but presently, breaths bathed anticipatorily, coming events adequately suited doing Mentone society very good vibrancies, currently, most important issues concerned erecting more towers after many's construction, not minding whether similar edifices already erected, far outnumbered Loving's entire population –this being third day New Loving's construction commenced.

Thirty minutes succeeding work commencements, little Debbie, acquiescing upon Victoria's prompts, decided playing devil's advocate, by suggesting building picket fences between every residential manor, or each family's houses, or better yet, residences interested family hoped snagging. Picket fences notably absentee'd profiles augmenting Mentone homes, no one anticipated interfering neighbors, locals seldom quarreled living around each other, yet, none fathomed why Debbie dutifully educated men laboring -on anticipated events accompanying oncoming futurities times seemed nigh -too soon unawares upon people, saying– ways change, folks adopt new styles, contrasting civic methods, approached, perhaps inculcated within culture, fears regarding growing introvertedness amongst locals broadened: completely dissociating one's self socially –should drastic times beckon measures equally pathetic, arguing– no better ideas existed beyond integrating picket fences between homes during constructing residences around New Loving's suburbs, Debbie's furthering argument convinced attentive but hesitant workmen:- during coming eras, as seen through rabbit holes –all people encountered daily are neighbors that all but acquired generally broadened scopes incorporating better choices, begun desiring demarcating-fences between neighbors, following persistent confusion, Debbie sought insights into suitable modern county house architecture beyond increasingly exhibiting private homes' demarcation profiles prior– or succeeding construction? -earned concord.

Ensuingly - once jobbers agreed, each resumed working ensuring continuing work slightly altered blueprints plans henceforth incorporated single family houses' accommodations, demarcated by hitherto unaccepted features. Men-built inch after inch, whilst murmuring themselves encouragements -how each craves proving commitment if any possessed any worth, how if any collective strengths persisted; altogether, each, bar-none intended giving building whole nine yards, completely disregarding constant warnings by school teachers exhibiting understandings-working too hard oftentimes caused health detriments, each simply - almost as pugnacious as possible, hunched over, working, apparently, each hoped impressing unutterable arbitrary thoughts on warrioresses? --no ideas! -but- viabilities could later give.

"Say– who's with any justifiable suppositions?" -queried little Debbie, sincerely expecting reliable responses colleagues readied offering, following great friendships developing. Given experiences fraternizing, enabling peers nearer adopting profitable ideas already titillating minds, others must abide by, became one habit learned,

"Make yourself clearer–" -miss Van Linden inquired right back,

"I mean– look how hard our boys work themselves, I doubt if all twenty five alliance fellows really satisfy families this much -look how many houses we have already, yet are three days along, several more foreshadowing project's scheduled end,"

"I reckon some truths– little wonder if any ever do assignments once school closes, nor help doing household chores –each's present over exertion shows–?"

"Your guess equates mine, Victoria, beats me, maybe, alliance working men love assistive roles,"

"I haven't an inkling, maybe soon, we'll find proper ways we'd repay any good, cash demands clearly skipped boy's minds –we hadn't forecasted any such plans anyhow –we'll figure matters out,"

"Any preferences? –short hangouts, perhaps longer ones?" Debbie inquired, optimistic Victoria's response provides much needed insights, somewhat afraid expressing premeditation as concisely as adults, infringed sensibilities,

"I usually prefer idling away hours entertaining friends, close friends certainly make good outing fellows -even if I have all weekend, my preferences includes lazying around through rests, enjoying folks' warmth," Victoria replied, moments later, refocused attentions on workingman, since continuing discussions over working men's demands soon after work closes, seemed an unnecessary extension of work into after hours.

Seventy, eighty, over one hundred-perhaps more houses by twenty, entered final construction stages after which, construct many more around areas designated suburbs. Mentally premising alliance men's entrance clutching panhandling hats, project initiator apprised of Victoria's suggestions awaiting better prepared paymasters, held back moments after overtly professing inadequacies-flashing dashing smiles after dashing smile excepting one toothless one-flaunted by whom shall-n't be identified--appreciative fellows owed outstanding debts contained, opining– not after disproportionately strenuous work involving vigorously earth pounding, bare knuckles sore, dirtied feet stamping terra firma hard, ensuring construction pressed ahead smoothly. Openly hoping neither rain nor flood revisited soon, most sensible ones pointed out desires within every heart, each secretly wanted shareholder's statuses by whatever means regarding whatever proceeds-proprietor, or plural thereof-should Victoria have become equal partners –set eyes upon-launching on-going initiative, but presently, either held onto presuppositions workingmen retained cool attitudes until time appropriately sanctioned transiting between calm collectedness as well as unruly demanding natures, endeavors equaledn't adventures –giving uttermost concentrations, attacking earth unrelentingly –that much audacity ordinarily ranked each amongst deserving people.

Upon terminating this third day's work, Ms. Van Linden-as usual, made announcement little Debbie–as did all eighteen 'workingmen' boys heretofore not reneged on work ethic, heeded,

"I must depart," working girl's second ranking official announced moments after spying Van Linden's obtuse vehicles approaching in surrounding southward distance, given rearing, prepared departing on Linden Oil's Cadillac limousine parking; on Van Linden automobiles halting completely, Victoria boarded without further ado, winked one last time as windows rolled up.

Disengaging automobile's brakes, Cuthbert Dilsomeworth maneuvered around its padded stirring wheel, ensuring family's carriage scooted away-taking group's de facto number two along appropriate directions - till next occasion work resumed around hours counting not beyond sixteen, or next morning's 8, or nine'ish o'clock. Such, starting during incipience became cliché, whenever work finished, Victoria departed hurriedly, leaving Debbie attending workingmen company lonesomely.

On this third day, Debbie, concentrating more on kind words, encouraged finishing off whatever job remained, as time hurriedly approached dismissals-half hour remaining, several took time professing increasingly feeling underneath bad weathers; no doubt, swashbuckling persona's observed earlier on - abandoned each last one, over-exertion having taken tolls, little Debbie decided circumstances warranted quitting day's endeavors, another minute, legends surrounding 'proverbial last straws' workingmen's spirits broke upon, manifests.

UNEXPLAINED VISITORS

Fear, perhaps real dread? -no, more like awe, gripped all Loving's townships, as edifices on Mentone's prime location-rumors swirled around County increasingly approached skywards–but-judge Trimble's orders! --holding unshakably, none else save Debbie's crew approached Beacon Light hoping catching glimpses or finding out actual transpirations fueled undying talk around county's seven towns -whose main topics initially centered broadly on girls doing wondrous stuff, but diligent spooks intent on returning news: accurate, maybe not, variously disclosed numerous instances showing boys steady gazing, suggested about one hundred-perhaps two - young men-earth over sent hither--agents reported within information returned, or seventy, busied themselves toiling away tirelessly under stringent supervision by two unidentified female county executives, perhaps petroleum bigwigs? -or land grabbers? -no one could certainly bet on recognizing indictable identities additionally circulating throughout grapevines, other pressing matters included issues surrounding spooks' preferential strategies gathering returned information—sometimes narrated audiences wearing straight faced unblinking eyes, undetected, operatives artfully interposing great distances between secretive agencies detailed by several county executives supposedly observing all one hundred or more workingmen entire universe detailed, alongside many detailed by various towns comprising Loving, properly depicting individual facial features on seventy hard working folks strenuously erecting suburban buildings containing living spaces, offices, plus many optional features some proprietress believed civilized housing projects human inhabitation deserved, required -using desert sands – everyone ought solicit.

Matters bettered, regarding others --depending on whose perspective-worsened, once current Loving's mayor-narrative still refuses identifying, else– issued corroborative order cordoning off all roads converging roads, preventing automobile traffic approaching Debbie's estates. Mayor's orders imputed police activities, as well as sheriff department's blockades; cordoning off roads successfully ending entire Mentone's traffic, ensuring virtually all township parts experienced gloomy atmospheres brought on by forlornness due scanty movements around town, or non-visitations thereof, consequently help matters greatly - enabling construction attain break neck speeds no less.

During team's rendezvous one day following Victoria's sudden departure passing uneventfully excepting longing ogles meted by all sixteen workingmen, following third day's original count dwindling by two, exact digits obtained during onsets tallied twenty five or -six, handfuls:–presently-sixteen 'resilient's', later reported as capturing mindfulness –swore oaths conveying resolute determinations until construction finishes, shortly afterwards, another unknown young miss-emerging wheresoever, approached site, without anyone's invitation nor permission, invariably encouraging workingmen's assumption confrontations awaited either little Debbie, Ms. Victoria separately, or together-if club ordinances permitted, others gazed on, forgoing raising probing voices thereby halting progressing but unhurried steps,

"We're familiar–" one boy disclosed not certain anyone overheard, hyperventilations indicating fatigue brought on by continued all around weighted sand excavation hard working boys readily moved about, graciously allowing even more feature filled buildings, but also anxiety, "Miss Ravenshield, or Culverwell," -another noted, "I can't quite remember precisely, we do relate sometimes,"

"Right-" replied Tripwith Shillingsford, Jonathan Ramsbottom just negotiated girl's identity,

"Perfect by me If Miss Ravenshield, or Culverwell, joins ranks," peer replied, thereafter, master Shillingsford's conversational remarks addressing Jonathan Ramsbottom's interests continued-though subdued, leaving workingmen obfuscated ensuing apropos palaver's contents, else assume laziness emerging, nor relented -leaving others greater travails.

Debbie stood arms akimbo, paying Miss Mogridge's remarks good heed as opposed continuing on little chitchats involving Victoria, though proceeded soon anyhow,

"Do we expect rendezvous tonight? -no particular time yet, but tonight, do I understand correctly?" Little Debbie craved accurate information as– truths alone enabled better uninterrupted choices; buildings, edifices, houses used as private domiciles alongside office blocks constructed here, fabrications never profited anyone, such personal styles pleased neither Debbie nor Victoria's adoptive sensibilities,

"Yes, tonight," replied miss Mogridge answering little Debbie's inquiry, ensuring replies conveyed across some seriousness project's hosts expected, after all, counting subjective diligences–as legend interpreted during later eras, too- played advanced roles during redevelopments --but accepted town's officially detailed duties otherwise-possible - gathering relatable information returnable as credible facts project's VIP worked with.

Ensuant conversation revealed much; little Debbie made judicious surmisals-Zoe hadn't any knowledge individuals accompanying upcoming visitors, nor possessed any suitable warnings every girl possibly-fostering remote involvements building prospective 'Phoenix rising', sought after –once overheard in-between folks': Adrian Mogridge during night time discussions, Zoe imbibed through keen attention, intending making discoveries whereupon acquired information Archibald Mogridge passed Agnes Mogridge -concerning mysterious men perhaps women's impending visits, plans included determining goings-on whereabouts loving; '*august visitors*', –such appellations Debbie knew, befitted strange people arriving Loving County--not New Loving, suddenly.

Miss Mogridge's timely call on cavorting dear fellow friendly warrioresses: Debbie accompanying peer Victoria, reporting imminent occurrences–believed may suitably prep many ahead encountering strange fellows - should certain folks' determinations perchance permit beating all odds-blockaded streets posed– suddenly appearing during continuing work, earned good approvals.

Little Debbie usually frowned upon truancy -never sneaking outside Charibert-family house–whatever case crops up; be temptation adventures or fun, unfailingly informed mother, whenever father disappointed similar indulgences, impelled on Mrs. Charibert's assistance requesting Buchard Mr. Charibert's permits endorsing lengthy stays outdoors, neither Buchard–not Ayleth ever foiled hopes, constantly allowing ward obtain required permission afore encountering interesting diversions outdoors, but on this occasion, unprecedented as Charibert's households youngest folk, important house rules wore out, Little Debbie's presumption father: Buchard Charibert accompanied by unhappy county officials planned purposeful Beacon Light visitation whereupon sternly instill corrective attitude. Time passed slowly till closing time arrived on dusk's swift wings, no adults, including well acquainted ones, successfully circumvented Trimble' orders yet.

Moderately past 10 PM tomorrow, little Debbie, assured father busied self-fast asleep alongside mother, quickly disembarked long assisting cradle, put-on tight-fitting jeans overall underneath thick hooded sweaters, relinquishing thoughts inclement weather forecasted approaching weather deteriorations. Peeking through glass windows adorning bedroom's wall right after playfully dusting debris off inspirational Lego City Buchard Charibert installed on fifth birthday - complimenting sleep chamber architecture, tired eyes beheld familiar night sights-predominantly deepened shadows, surrounding all over, perfect timing Debbie adjudged - suiting covert adventures outside any menage?

Quick deliberations on appropriately departing, eventually influenced going out through bedroom's solitary window, utterly disregarding associated risks; dangers always accompanied climbing ladders; one-falling off, another breaking one's legs - often occurring nearly every time teenage someone's consider descending downstairs through sometimes unstable ladders, awakening whilst surgery mending broken limbs proceeds, constituted repeating thoughts, upon self-advisement-as demonstrated, determined ill preparedness. Yet another means perfectly easy egress regularly occurred , being simple walk outs through either doors entering or exiting Charibert's; back door mainly - if stealthy egress counted more - as Buchard Charibert's self-installed front doors creaked noisily each time anyone entering or departing thrust one ajar, but, 23 Pecos street's rear entrance door, creaked too - not mightily –tad audible extents, waking slumbering folks up, threatened. Leaving through finished basement's door, tallied third as yet another means, but sometimes, keys weighed much, clanging clamorously each time Ayleth or Buchard opened doors, however, granted tonight's perambulations, heavy basement keys sufficed as best bets.

Exercising test iterations, Debbie stealthily entered bungalow's backyard parts seeking chilled breeze, successful tack eliminating clatter employed involved clutching individual keys apart, then tightly together preventing annoying clanging, whilst inserting corresponding keys against door's unlock chink, basement doors colluded successfully, emitting little creaky sounds outbound girl's ears barely heard, ergo– earned best bet, little else apropos choices remained; ladders surreptitiously lowering one downstairs-risking falling, snapping ankles, then shattering night's stillness howling—enabling folks catch one in sneaking off acts-until moments leading into pain induced screams, wished secretive, or-- creaky back doors, or front doors responsive if clamorous keys once perceived making joyous noises meeting keyholes whilst unfastening met keyholes, but tonight, if basement doors may well silently usher Debbie outside en-route Beacon Light, beats curiosities just yet.

Penultimate fifth day construction events commenced through Debbie's tonight's transgressions, another eight hours would see work end-reaching construction's termination points, all required edifices-standing tall. Time ticked 10:24 p.m. Charibert's bungalow through Debbie's perception distances away, lay absolutely quiet, isolated tick tocks produced by several clocks hung on walls nevertheless shattered calm atmospheres by imbuing lively sounds about. Everything else remained positioned as elder Chariberts' stowed; seats, chairs, entertainment centers housing memories containing Buchard Charibert's youth; one stereo sitting beside TV screen purchased decades previously, an old telephone set fondness compelled Charibert's retention: long serving Chariberts –virtually becoming family, but moreover, worked like new.

Little Debbie made initial moves locating appropriate keys on one long owned oak stands situated between two entry ways advancing on elder Charibert's chambers. First, Debbie peered through glass patches on basement's door, sadly beholding shady unilluminated outsides, indeed ominous darkness exclusively extended everywhere, yet invitingly beckoned Debbie Charibert as slender fingers fussed over each other binding several keys; one, or two, all thirty-together using blue painter's masking tapes, effectively preventing clatter, this essential exercise finished successfully shortly, leaving solo - one key marked similarly as inscriptions appearing on door's chink--forcing basement's door yield outsides. Yield outsides, basement door proved capable - once Debbie inserted appropriately inscribed key #7, ushering Mentone's daring warrioress outside into deepened umbra, without second thoughts, little Debbie Charibert-shutting basement door behind, , as consequent result, proceeded without another moment's hesitation or thought concerning imminencies inside Mentone's darkness, thankfully, persistent silence surrounding Debbie's activities, left sleeping folks unperturbed.

Bewildered over reasons unannounced guests - Zoe warned everyone chose visiting, or forebodings locals ought expect as respects New Loving's newest edifices, Debbie's crucial decision providing Beacon Light chief warrioresses' presence under any circumstances, but most probably chose personally safeguarding everything warrioresses assisted by 'Loving Boys Alliance', managed erecting, should upcoming aforementioned transients precisely consists wholly or partly: one spectacular disheartening teardown by Emmett Booth's caterpillar assisted by ever ready Eardwulf Thornwood intently casting haunting imageries involving huge seven feet caterpillar rollers or tracks, flattening little erected edifices, or running unsuspecting younger folks over.

Appearing particularly true, Miss Charibert minded troubling objections, as little by little, corner after corner, little Debbie Charibert proceeded till Beacon Light greeted bleary views --upon arrival encountered strange sights representing unknown fellows whom no Mentonian nor any inhabiting county's disparate parts ever visited, sustained any knowledge of, nor ever seen previously.

Strangers Loving's darkness harbored stood distances away, ten yards adjacent nearest New Loving's east side known between all *WG* Sorority, plus any other involved: as Lego city, though hewed uncouthly using nature's most prevalent matter. Her balls rolled perfectly, understanding situations really well; as owner, institutor - proprietor -as appropriately alluded by everyone knowledgeable, situation required presence by one significant operative involved, Loving county generally needed countering every actions land grabbing mysterious strangers silhouetted not quite thirty yards abreast Lego city's eastern most parts, more or less seemed like one or two additionally cast images of fiends about exacting unenviable outcomes on everyone's strenuous endeavors.

Emboldened, little Debbie decided unidentified lunatics must presume possessing magisterial authorities flouting county court orders, wherefore deserved braving forced discontinuance, notwithstanding values costing an arm, arms, maybe legs, nothing about New Loving accurately enunciated unmanageable endeavors, no person possessing rudimentary knowledge pertaining Little Debbie Charibert, supposes weakness anyhow? –questionable odd authorities once presumes imbued naysayers understandings building edifices solely belonged as reserves big conglomerates monopolized? -times have changed, all little girls - should succinct knowledge be eluding cynics, matured shrewdly, ever becoming dangerous–even if by gradual imperceptible ways, rightfully overbearing, heroics, oftentimes hyper aggressive: precisely, incorporated within imminent actions hyper aggressive defeatist killjoys ought witness soon - should impending appearances entail approach commencing Lego city's tear down, or unauthorized enjoyment, or claims, or claims assertions as comprising part, surpassed hyper aggressiveness certain government personnel thrived on. Almost vainglorious-exhibiting Motorola handset readily, not as weapon strangers presently occupying Mentone's darkness deserved confronting, but geared toward emergency SOS's, summoning powerful local Admiral Sagard Summers, obviously perceived powerful but most importantly, plus any others not readily off noggins presently --Debbie approached one whose poised betrayed as night shadow silhouette's leader, remarkably true-warrioress's determination proved –encounter's unknown figure eagerly engaging Debbie's conversations commencing briefly, indeed affirmed leadership,

"Little girl," solemnly commenced presumed leader's gruff voice on this first instance talking, warrioress immediately guessed strange unfamiliarity about its inflection: no one ever spoke thus consonantally anymore, vocals sounded way– natural, friendly, brotherly-yet powerful lonesome girl almost apprehended uncertain impressions– Meanwhile, darkness' leading man continued, interrupting thoughts briefly, "I am Oliver Loving, I hath commenced Loving, I hath 'arriv-' thither thee-thank as thou may'st progress beyond whence I hath ceased eons ago,"

"I miss comprehensions on your references; Oliver Loving? Oliver Loving? -famed Oliver Loving, legends suppose founded Loving County? –Oliver Loving-Loving County establisher approaching two centuries ago?" -inquired incredulous Debbie transitorily wondering if continuing demonstrations - went without being clever scenes perfunctorily enacted by strange impostors,

"I am," -acknowledged most front oriented silhouette's gruffy voice Debbie still couldn't identify facially, "I hath Oliver Loving, I hath established cá en 1866 ans upon times aborigines assayed de tué cá de moi, mais-- as hospitable place le-gens may'st visit…"

Warning bells somehow stimulated suspicions, sounding off piercingly within Debbie tout de suite; once-not too long ago, Debbie sought explanations why peaceful places often came under attack, then, questions remained pertaining night time stranger's incredulous claims none else established Loving, not New Loving anyhow, lastly, clarifications on Loving's supposedly establishing 'Loving County as hospitable place conducingly welcoming –had Oliver Loving apprehended flood riders not long ago…

Notwithstanding, Mentone's night time's stranger continued, "thank benign creators on high, I hath vanquished les, ét voilà, Loving! Tonight, I hath many thanks, merci thee all--"

"Oh my!" -exclaimed little Debbie Charibert shivering–mostly cold, but afraid too –standing still thoroughly misapprehended currently unfolding event, besides being uncertain encounter's entailments truly involved inopportunely meeting acclaimed historic figures bearing faces southern traditions themselves concealed-centuries going; Ayleth advised taking adults' dispensed insights lightly, perhaps this perfectly represented such situations as continuance furthered –keen eyes witnessed seven silhouettes conversing through pantomimes Debbie thought each barely saw. Inept over shadowy figures' pantomimes, little Debbie chinwagged front most silhouette conveying leader's gruffy voice, "–whereas 'Oliver Loving' as your remarks indicates– say, do say– why companions surrounding thee-if 'companions', discuss by pantomimes, do speech impediments deprive your group simple commentary?"

"My men resists shattering umbra's prevalent stillness, New Loving continues hallowed being contemporaneous Phoenix rising this modern era, as I hath cá envisaged one century or more ago."

Perfect logic existed around Loving's Lego City references as hallowed grounds, Debbie's trepidation simmered knowing figures-if as touted, exited one century past onto tonight's occasion, bore New Loving towers many filibusterings, bad weather, floods everyone theoretically knows - persuaded erecting, some kind words

"Hallowed grounds, ey?" -Little Debbie later recounted tonight's exploits privileged writers-hoping presumptions proves authentic, made subject matter of countless unpublished manuscripts deserving publication,

"Hallowed grounds!" -replied Loving hoping kind words still mattered much nowadays -as one strange night time girl: assuming Oliver Loving's apprehensions proved right, engaged one mysterious fellow: Oliver Loving-if considering Debbie's own premises. Interesting facts laced further interlocutions, till Loving's six accompanying silhouettes sauntered off, beginning inspecting, or re-inspecting building after building, edifice after edifice, feature after features-embedded within structure after structure within little Debbie Charibert's Lego city, upon completing distinct tasks, re-engaging encounter's initial speaker another silhouette addressed presently as 'master', after inspecting every last nook accentuating modernity into all Lego city's crannies, argued quietly among themselves, this time, silhouettes spoke vocally upon instruction by gang's front man circumspection indeed introduced Debbie Charibert as truly Oliver Loving, but still, conversed conspiratorially consequently rendering audibility impossible beyond few yards,

"Stupid old men–" cursed Debbie breathlessly -how toplofty gossiping by figures alike out seeking undue requisitioning, hurt!

One, obviously striking Debbie as pretentiousness engaging pointless talking as though matters excluded one lone girl facing eight men somewhere inside Loving county's gloom, rational dictated everyone conversing needed equal participation, after all, New Loving came about-none else's, not even Oliver Loving's, hers alone - hers-effectively luring goons emerging past eras back inside Loving vicinities tonight; however, supposing silhouetted pack's truer identities mismatched Oliver Loving's, easily rendering satisfactory attributes as 'criminals' impersonating great historic figures as grand designs sinister group availed themselves efforts fashioning inroads about Lego city-little Debbie invested every efforts bring alive, however, those disparaging comments one silhouettes keen hearing capture some strange unaccompanied little night time girl utter whisperingly, apparently hurt, thoroughly preventing comprehending why aspersions were cast, researched estimations accordingly showed - impertinence never once proved productive - regretted Debbie almost self-recriminatingly, as- impertinence thoroughly lacked dynamism consistently fronted by warrioresses, represented, no wise person ever auspicated rudeness versus strangers during initial night time's encounter, none correctly guessed unacceptable behaviors --none purposed interceding-should strangers have come, preparing-forceful usurpation, or plunder?

-twenty six 'alliance men?' -what diddly-squats tarnishes good reputations permanently above sloth? –would twenty unruly boys whose presence alone instigates negativity within sides manifest terribly as bare-knuckled fist fighting, showcase tireless Tripwith Shillingsford's main skills anyhow, or– boisterous Jonathan Ramsbottom's? --No doubt advantageously protected by parent's cozy home sleeping - after melancholic lullaby succeeded by sweet bedtime stories administered lulls- Really, pointlessness vain glorious attempts during inopportune hours stared starkly, strong worded exchanges one positioned group's rightward third-but on Loving's left uttered-another put up with, apparently reached lone observer's hearing across night's serenity, moments later, howled vociferously-shattering all stillnesses about, foreboding corrections-should venturesomeness compel more utterances, Debbie's immediate anxiety seriously took account silhouetted group discerned '*stupid old men*' slur - not quite many seconds ago:, each must have heard uttered–

'Guess what'd look good on one young visage staring defying darkness bound men?' -questions imagined next, echoed within Debbie's mind, "my slap on your pretty young face," answers exiting query's source, echoed within as well. During fleeting moments finding more tolerable responses; little Debbie's self-advisement duly suggested phlegmaticness, 'penny given your thoughts' -heartfelt admonishments echoed within, "imprudence benefits little-I say, being difficult during such hour-lounging around strange men presumed passed over periods besting one hundred-fifty years ago, learned era-bound wisdoms pertinent era tales sustained --no doubt, assault across Debbie's pretty face imbues more insult where dwells injury - following speculations usurping Lego City besides New Loving holding premiere positions within land grabber's ends, such rendered any attempts or maneuvers redressing any unpalatable actions unfeasible –anyways, unambitious others eventually go about alluding classifications as 'little spoiled brat' utterly lacking proper upbringing, or heed established boundaries, Debbie Charibert resignedly accepted compelling logics inherent within immediate situations, 'act thusly, one'll end up one wiser…'

"Cease noise! Else that shall be ours tonight-" rude stranger uttered additionally; Debbie heeded unsure which promised becoming their tonight, none else, or New Loving just abreast over –but on peering closer whereupon sighted man's outstretched hand indicating New Loving estates direction, realized.

Thank goodness, matters never reached uncomfortable heads, for– moments later–maybe several, miss Charibert witnessed all eight silhouettes turn around without another word, thereafter began undertaking treks advancing departure, then rapidly diminished as repeating steps conveyed all eight further away- uncanny movements manifested extremely unnaturally, making deeming 'ghosts' upon figures constituting diminishing apparitions proper, soon afterwards turned around too-welcoming departures. Hurriedly, Debbie inspected most Lego City's 70 yd.^{2} –determining no harm, ventured away, backtracking towards Charibert residences, little Debbie geared little steps thrown after small ones towards 23 Pecos Street.

Notwithstanding countless fables, historical proof Loving indeed existed, incontrovertibly survives; same Oliver Loving - whose legacy carries till date on beautiful bald eagle's wings, as Debbie trekked back allowing wonderments on sudden unfolded eventuality -certainly, much diligences required consideration if any real historical re-evaluation ought come about.

Careful scrutiny up ahead along Pecos' furthest parts revealed one reddish night time automobile perceived abandoned immediately upon turning corners resembled Jimmy Wescotte Charibert's, elder sibling, not much lay beyond younger Mr. Charibert's devices rutting capabilities - given unhinged tires, worn nuts or indeterminate faults eventually substantiating brother Wescotte's decisions abandoning prized possessions, given several characteristics Wescotte's old Chevy flaunted, undoubtedly appearing too imperfect, inspecting evidently unstable vehicle hoisted on bricks, could keel perilously causing bodily harm despite affording old faithful extensive modifications, since no diverse other ways sustaining injuries-inspecting abandoned automobiles could help circumstances, wherefore avoided initiating any risky activity –Wescotte's Old faithful wouldn't quit faltering--similarly repeating shortcomings once again tonight,

"Oh well," fumed Debbie, times are nigh one should no longer consider circumstances engulfing Wescotte's forgotten transport-hers--or Loving's most immediate concerns, still, rationale dictated helping find more suitable places deserving abandonment. Quicker steps settled more land distance, unsure certain muffled sounds auditory nerves interpreted incorrectly, permeated Loving's disappearing gang now far gone beyond one hundred yards' immediate surroundings –or perhaps some un-depicted faceless one nearby gave sound rise. Frightened, Debbie put feet: left versus right, right upon left's usage repeatedly, rapidly succeeding each other, as flight enabled deliverance beyond harm's reach-till 23 Pecos loomed underneath Mentone's darkened skies.

After expertly meandering through mostly unlit Mentone, perceived Charibert's silhouetted afar - as bungalow's form materialized. Familiar domiciles soon welcomed its own-as quietly as exiting an hour-not quite two ago. Once basement door shut behind Debbie, nimble fingers unwound singular keys previously bound together effectively preventing dissonant cacophony small metals often produced. Quickly retraced steps provided by tired feet, saw Debbie up inside assigned sleep chambers upstairs minutes later-clocking 2:05.a.m. --re-immersing therein familiar pleasures one's living quarters always afforded, thereafter, joined humanity's well-deserved rest.

PLOT THICKENS

    Scarcely one week following Debbie initiating construction, two or more families, searching out better prospects not found anywhere else, suspecting better prospects locals ought avail themselves –or perhaps simply dwell amidst civilization, perhaps advancement, existed elsewhere - not Mentone or surrounding Loving county townships, vacated town –reaching greener pastures big city Austin Texas fabled as beckoning too hard soon enough-offered, others pitched ideas upon folks realigning places alongside parent's domiciles once abandoned, numerous suppositions propounded such persons usually found gainful employment with any of many natural gas places across Texas, possessed much expendable cash, ergo– could not have been due widespread impoverishment – mindful conditions generally missed Mentone, Loving County or elsewhere around by wide margins, those revered barons guaranteed employment working fuel wellsprings harvesting crude someone placed beneath earth's bowels during prehistory, creating permanent income yielding livelihoods locals hoped on. While Loving's sister towns housed sparse population, temporary daily entrants' wealthy corporations reserved lucrative work contracts working oil derricks, far outnumbered local populations by ten hundred percents, approximately reaching five times; not- Mentone, not Loving's remaining seven towns, but entire county's population.

    Little Debbie's entire family never arranged moving elsewhere, not least Debbie, until time passes, Loving's Mentone promised remaining everyone's hometown, exactly when sooner-or later warrioresses boast-'ed' distinct successes garnered through New Loving, as hour after hour on Monday --construction's final day, rolled by, Debbie, alone today following Vicky Van Linden's wake reporting ill: truly stricken ill, following three more alliance working men dropping out, another two dilly-dallying after promising work site visits soonest, but wouldn't, leaving sixteen hands on deck this closing day.

One after another, alliance men successfully terminated particular tasks, picking up spades, shovels, diggers, latterly acquainting taskmaster Charibert required reports, as certain boys five yards - huddled together admiring cumulative day's work erecting an entire county replica comprising seven surrounding towns on Mentone's Beacon Light.

Long minutes passed silently without anyone mustering courage-but gaze upon victory. Once trepidations diminished, one uttered moments later,

"My-oh-my! -little Debbie!" -exclaimed that one, "-whatsoever are our eyes bringing upon our visions?"

"Little Debbie's Lego city," chorused three amidst teeming alliance men, several auditory encounters including 'Little Debbie's Lego city', firmly entrenched within several psyches as most viable title New Loving estate could bear, however, more titles awaited New Loving could bear once deemed more appropriate,

"Lend me your ears fellows-" little Debbie began addressing excited alliance, "soonest after localities resumed normal activities following several brown outs, I shall have an offer-" Alliance boys-too impatiently awaiting further briefing, wanted put through shortly,

"Say-" demanded one currently suffering tricks maturity often played on young insensible boys, Debbie heeded, accordingly informed 'alliance men' sisterhood's policies already accommodated each person's salaries, available once humanity resumed relocating back-

"I shall figure out enumerations due each hardworking alliance men, even if many dropped out recently, keep fingers crossed."

Indeed, announcing remittable salaries addressing exerted labor, augured working men some relief, few however preferred settlements unorthodoxly: each hoped earning rights permitting constant rendezvous alongside Debbie Charibert promenading New Loving's neighborhoods -seen by peers whilst holding Debbie during interesting duologues, as promenades proceed along shores, lake waters originating sea breezes bathing two warm skins partly exposed underneath apparels, someone spoke-briefly shattering fantasies scores envisioned flourish within,

"Maybe, keeping friendly company more often, as opposed working like events around here lately, we could drop by events nearby towns host, we'd love your company venturing about Debbie as payment–" -deepening apprehensions various still uncertain's nursed, quickly broadened even more on ideas constituting previously mentioned alternate remittances,

"Wonderful idea–Debbie, really," promises reverberated, "fix dates, or occasions-if any, I'm quite sure I'll visit each,"

Agreeable promises settled contentiousness - given many clamoring interests, boys screeched joyfully, apparently, earning one's labor's worth despite being each attendant preteen lad's age, counted significantly -each relished accompanying Debbie about, rendering lucky ones - within certain onlooker's perspectives -as much Mentone celebrities as Debbie Charibert herself, but until circumstances warrant private promenades. Once ululations ceased, alliance's Radnor vowed on peer's behalf -optimistically pledging continued silences-as much as several registered as drop-outs evidently managed, still– given Townsend's findings, no one disavowing court any authorities, risked paying Beacon Light's newest estate unwarranted visits; subsequently, scope out results back breaking labor begat, or hamper accumulating progress, or render stoppages anyhow, bearing Townsend's news, Debbie, supervising minority work alliance fellows totally psyched over building Loving minding objectives far beyond erecting buildings, or associate closer later on –each certainly hoped little Debbie Charibert understood –professed Trimble-whose judicial orders stayed everyone away, easily compelling unmitigated Beacon Light abstinence, none whatsoever encroached work site, or zone, much gratitude using succinct appellation: *'Loving's 'real' hero'*

–none cared about serving sentences inside penitentiaries across unknown places as recompense each thankful one's hunches sees as certainly redressing contrarinesses - no one wished risking, locals could afford staying away above spending months on end serving callous penitentiaries whims' somewhere–

Time gained upon all - infusing within each great nostalgia folk's whereabouts often imbued, Debbie-through handshakes, acknowledged motivated stout hearted alliance personal convictions New Loving truly worth every moment spent erecting associated towers. One particular motivated boy-needlessly identified, on one moment's spur, indeterminately resolved instituting ceremonies commemorating collective triumph, as everyone else prepares making similar suggestions once opportunities offer themselves, Debbie inarguably understood likely suggestions permeating talk about town upon admissions --none knew comparable exploits elsewhere: new habitable abodes materializing - like nothingness suddenly began bearing fruits -but through its resident's own young children's bare knuckles.

Maddened excitedly, thirteen individuals still writhed, expending continuous energy rebuilding New Loving, proudly gasconading can-do attitudes, awaiting more New Loving inauguration strivings, totally endorsing Debbie's ideas, each waited-several minutes -almost five, no soul outside immediate gatherings deserved appropriating whatever credits triggered by formally creating awareness folks-perhaps luminaries dependent on developments wanted.

One contentious issue however sprang up almost immediately: whose name, or names or titles as articulated, most befitted assigning towering edifices, various roads, or streets crisscrossing Loving,

"Mine, mine," declared amply zealous Radnor Townsend observing quick responses forestalling rivalrous boy's preemptive response, "grab onto mine Debbie, mine outclasses everyone else's- mine's far most beautiful–" -on Debbie's inquisition: requesting quickly viewing specifics Radnor Townsend deemed 'Beautiful', Debbie Charibert heard;

"Radnor Townsend lakefront Avenue!"

"Certainly – young-Townsend-sir," -agreed Debbie, "Radnor Townsend lakefront Avenue! -Names given after thee-your fashioned shall henceforth assume," -Debbie Charibert's promises gingered others up, few then gallivanted about proudly declaring family names repeatedly, as per agreement, elicited clarifying conditions, "put another way, unique labeling shall exist along spots attended continually by each till finish points, roads besides towers or homes attributed individuals efforts," continued Debbie, "Radnor worked alongside all on commencement right through till present," -explanations–encouraged by audiences' rapt attention, continued, as dextromanuals index finger indicated New Loving's parts oriented furthermost anent south, north heading-as noted, towards Beacon Light open waters, "Lakefront Avenue as originally name conjoins 'Radnor Townsend's name - becoming - Radnor Townsend lakefront Avenue! --Agreed?"

Requiring more sensible arguments, Radnor Townsend's peers all agreed, areas one lent efforts developing henceforth assumed such person's choice designations, permanently altering lakefront Avenue's designation into:- *'Radnor Townsend'* everyone till date supposes good enough.

Quite disappointed given another's preemptive strike, Quinnell Keighleyworth almost similarly attired as Radnor, coincidentally-or not, reprehensibly upped cordially continuing conversation to heated arguments between colleagues; timorous until today, seldom spoke even if questions came posed directly, sometimes --thanking no apparent reason, avoided peers, whenever addressed, pitched responses mostly constituting few words, but today, on account master Townsend poised emerging victorious over little Debbie's, intended speaking exhaustively, "Debbie, check mine out-if you please?" -inquired Quinnell Keighleyworth,

"Quinnell, yours? –Quinnell - I think–" Mr. Quinnell Keighleyworth heard Debbie retort right back,

"I am Quinnell, Quinnell Keighleyworth, take mine, sounds much appealing, school children's aural faculties'll handle mine better, I'm sure mine'll serve better traffic purposes if mainstay," pressed young Quinnell,

"All right Quinnell, let's see, let's see yours-"

Obviously wanting veritable titles, Quinnell Keighleyworth grabbed glad rags jeans pants waist band portions properly excluding boyish views, as if unbuckling– instead pulled upwards till protruding navels intervened –long sleeved right arm thrust deep inside pants pockets, retrieved parchment onlookers-on previous events mistook as greeting card, however contained inscriptions Quinnell hoped met standards therefore approval by little Debbie as 'lakefront's main avenue',

"My route deservedly earned better christening; Hoboken Drive," explained Quinnell thrusting parchment containing hand written '*Hoboken Drive*' inscriptions, forward,

"Hoboken Drive sounds awesome-Quinnell, very well, let's call yours Hoboken Drive, all right Quinnell Keighleyworth?" -Hoboken Drive Quinnell Keighleyworth's route became-on particular areas young mister Keighleyworth gave labor lifetime's best, until time passed henceforth, long after little Debbie's rise during later adulthood - ebbed, later resigning duties inside lone star state's hitherto unsung quarters' single-handedly instituted vision, Hoboken Drive conveniently stuck on hailing lips as:- 'Quinnell Keighleyworth' crescent connecting neighboring townships; Hay flat, Juanica, Mentone, Porterville, Ramsey, Red bluff reservoir, Woody- additionally, remained solely designated 'Quinnell Keighleyworth's road', Quinnell-on today's morning events concluding constructions, cleverly selected - by first willfully exchanging forceful opposing knuckles' bish-bash,

"See? -mine out-sizes by way– more, yours - I see is insignificant, verify forthwith, Ms. Debbie awaits," Quinnell taunted Radnor, "mine's reaches all six towns starting here, yours's specifically adjoins Shane's,"

"I bet we'll see about figuring stuff out!-Quinnell, I understand your qualms thoroughly,"

"Whatever! -please do revisit your drawing board; much work regarding better attitudes awaits," -mere awaiting promised artifices within opponent's capacity, young Mr. Townsend lured often reserved peer: Keighleyworth down antagonistic paths Debbie persistently discerned through decades hence.

Moments preceding heated arguments-briefly introduced speculations deleting names already christened alliance men-built roads, however-on second thoughts, citing needlessness worsening matters, quickly shelved inordinate actions, privilege-wise, each enjoyed owning likely named okay'd avenues, moreover, enterprisingly resolved accommodating rivalrous suitors-if not together, individually, leaving aside length issues commanded by streets graced by each builder's imposing efforts.

Disputatious working men grasped implications inherent within clarifications given; preferred names allotted individual's projects, met New Loving's requisites, hinting on why aggressing one another over one working girl's choice's sakes, deserved frowning upon, as– deserving attention equally-settling small concerns treating street designations, or selecting appellative identifiers, mattered too, Debbie decided mere civilities may not always warrant guarantees if conditions felt uncomfortable, however, Quinnell fit tad less perfectly as Radnor faired – though more willful courteously using *'please'* whilst supplicating.

'Sensitive–' as arguing fellows established over mistress' predictable presumptuousness gripping either side's-subjective efforts' tipped scales above rival's, pertinently therefore, entered zones innocence stuck fast merely on account each enjoyed familiarities spanning present times through second grade; one great quixotic triangle situation could have been: Debbie loved folks, eagerly joined classmates: boys or girls undertaking recreational activities, most decidedly, current rivalrous peers uncommonly monopolizing-therefore dedicating attentions-entirely on one or more pressing ideas -such thought patterns -mostly owing Radnor Townsend's perspectives, Quinnell's too, clearly upended foolishness, Debbie thought later upon fathoming individual standpoints,

"Fellows, I sound convincing, don't I?" -demanded Debbie Charibert, "both I mean-" -proud boys found throwing libations on friendship's alter over gaining warrior girl's attention, worthy,

"Cool," master Keighleyworth accepting little Debbie's injunctions, agreed, but wasn't really enough assuaging fixated angry stares, *'young Bessie Haynes males-'* -wondered Quinnell's date privately -really ought apprehend determined efforts well-meaning individuals hoped forestalled any threatening aggression, still–

"Boo–!" -hollered Townsend, displeased - project's main person now favored gazing upon rival.

HOME IS WHERE ONE'S HEART IS

  Implicit within orders issued by Trimble-suddenly designated 'good judge', world's best one, et cetera, lay several injunctions public trepidation looming imprisonment instilled, held perfectly, sustaining Debbie's ambitions, up till remarkable points - no local or guests dared advance anywhere near Beacon Light; court imposed moratorium, legislation's unforgiving weight, alongside 'log arms' every punitive law maintained, proved one great ally Mentone particularly, but Loving County generally, forbore charging; no list contained any known person maneuvering themselves around judicial injunctions, once one commits violations, society-must receive dues often through pricey corrective measures erring individuals suffers, Debbie acknowledged violating court orders injuncted by; county justice, judge, judicial official - disregarding appellations, or violator's status, wouldn't really matter, observable protocols often fell short encouraging continuance of ordinances: situation provoked law; once judges issued injunctions, or orders entered; county, or States, or federal court's records, thereafter-reaches appropriate governing agencies ratification, such as Trimble's order satisfied, becoming ordinance-everybody accepted - as folks currently abided by Trimble's.

  Debbie, one rainy morning later, recalled Mentone collectives-exiled - following unexpected floods-if one remembers correctly; arrived through rising water levels last night's deluge enveloped most Mentone by, essentially constituting third destructive floods all parts comprising Mentone but-miraculously, Beacon Light – whence quick flights took Debbie's whimpering self, seeking ascertainments New Loving still stood tall, which happily proved so --giving Debbie grounds for second quick but now exhilarated flight back 23 Pecos before Ayleth, perhaps Buchard discovered wards predawn exits. During these early stages, none could correctly guess whether said collectives comprised same unannounced visitation wealthy land grabbers driving expensive automobiles Charibert women spectated, accompanied by insincere politicians, or corrupt county executives

-speaking little about high state level counterparts, bringing up rears on waterlogged streets exacted months ago, or as many purposefully referenced ridiculously; '*visiting unwanted's, human flood*', or *land-grabbers* –but following reports certain locals unsurpassably gifted understating issues, submitted, no localities experienced any threats whatsoever as these nameless visitors' shoe soles wreaking ground borne havoc along chosen routes checking out Mentone, still-- most invariably reckoned peril coming small town Mentone's ways should assumptions determine erroneously. '*Suddenly, after hearing Mentone's magnificent lakefront erections solemnized moods between two beautiful but rival warrioresses - rendezvousing countless young men daily, witnessed relentless laboring*' thought Debbie satisfactorily, '*abandoners have returned.*'

Little Debbie Charibert's assistants: rich Ms. Victoria, aided by appurtenant assistants acting mostly on whims, caprices-even urges–reaching exceptional degrees most; Livilda, et al, hoped continued avoidance announcing or disclosing listings divulging warrioresses' identities, particularly - several others assigned special duties mandating secret meanderings about town, persisted, accordingly- kept personal identities as well as everyone's undisclosed, lest parents assume cross positions once offspring's are found toeing waterfront virgin's lines.

Myriad folks looked lots happier, peerless reasons accounting, pridefully carrying themselves about numerous life's supplemental endeavors --Loving County, as empty, as sparse, as underdeveloped as contrary localities remember, suddenly became familiar neighborhood once more - each onto populations last hoped returning someday. Indeed, Loving County-all laid back, remained homely like eras gone by –Unprecedented throughout Mentone's history, well-meaning citizens guised as working girls, unanimously decided premiere occasions instigating 'floods' comprising mostly locals, or natives diverse Loving county places listed as locals - resettling– yes, floods consisting humankind abandoning fragile windswept scrappy lives-unfortunate situations guaranteed each - as regrettably, all men must sooner or later, speak, or face truths –approach same origins-turbulent social currents swept many away-facing disordered places afar - Debbie needn't bother investigating as admission's prerequisites.

Warrioresses surmised reasons must have included though not solely such:- certain one's pronounced inability settling amidst welcoming communities elsewhere, Loving once again replaced words lips everywhere uttered joyfully as everyone turned around facing west, or east, north maybe-south, depending on geographical bearings life's pursuits deposited one, but generally directioned on returning paths - not least around surrounding towns, one everyone took stock-boasted residences incommensurably lack luster comparing erected Beacon Light marvels.

Self-asserting few inhabiting any Loving's towns listed above, as if validating capabilities, urgently summoned themselves; topics derived aside regular chitchats, treated making Lego City's most marvelous sections privy: parts befittingly opulent, New Loving authorities decided reserving enclaves none irrespective of status should approach, save passes enjoyed by few granted permission by ranking members, iffy observations on minds during these times-plentiful reactions militated against ubiquitous aches within locals desiring earnest endeavors resulted successes --notwithstanding successful candidates, providence ultimately graduates one onto master- or mistress-hood, perhaps mayor overseeing little Debbie's sand hewn Lego city, however valiant New Loving's builders make themselves.

Upon due time, viable remedies against self-denigration showcased, fascinating endeavors worth anticipating existed: as- tussling seeking proper habitat within 'any New Loving's most spectacular domiciles, as- instituting themselves deep inside goings-on thereabouts universe's most advanced parcel suddenly resideable by any. News locals reckoned finally filtered through, containing wee bit more juiciness, reached successful termination by Loving's most nondescript young daughters most notably one Ms. Debbie Charibert, although certain protagonists circulating titbits within nearly all current causeries'–consisting mainly rubbish information, dutifully exempted Debbie's parents: warrioresses perhaps benefited county wide corroboration keeping valuable news associating household's little one per lake front impressive exploits reaching all Loving County parents including Chariberts: quidnuncs also, should assumptions prove true, figured out identities notably names fitting linking several alliance devotees involved, rumor mill also expertly prevented distinguishing information reaching mothers, or fathers underneath whom spunky little child devotees: teeming alongside epoch's current children resentful of failures bordering on possible obtainments during older generations, let alone allow anyone discover young hands inserted inside cookie pots, exactly whilst corruption–or empty-handed or various distinctive unenterprisingnesses flourished. Per judge Trimble's continuing order, Debbie's alliance fellow: Quinnell Keighleyworth-whose wonderfully pieced avenues snagged selection based on lengths or breaths, or aesthetics, temporarily forsook Porterville during one event figuring like warrioress' most important rendezvous involving Debbie whereupon strolled along little Lego city's lengths. Row after row adorned by towers, castles, beautiful homes, streets after intersecting avenues welcomed former working associates-finally inseparable alongside what–if scaled life-size, approximated vast stretches, till- every indispensable monumental sight; offices, warehouses, factories, playgrounds-one finds nowhere else save Disney World - but belatedly augments New Loving's numerous monuments: brand new-though empty still whilst awaiting patronage-too, peculiarly entered account, all these, couple noted-promenade progressing, derived exclusively from one determined warrioresses' high-spirited almost scatterbrainedness attributed immaturity or improvidence towards discretion or proper sensibility's. Debbie Charibert leastwise, stubbornly insisted on accomplishments, here on this day, as Quinnell later intimated buddies –as very quickly accepting playmate's domineering personality without reservation as requisite snowballing relations further demanded -desire, as all boys struck by heartache knew through experience, determined never missing jolly boat rides on this one, hanging tough through thick, through thin till mounting raucous surrounding New Loving passes,

"Debbie, I sense significance approaching Loving," -exclaimed Quinnell, woefully making insufficient efforts keeping fidgety right palm holding companion's left, still. Debbie felt significant too-but reserved comments as day's most eventful trek down California's Hollywood Boulevard's equivalent: 'Memory lane' named after one alliance's workingmen: *Wedgeley T. Memory*, progressed, Quinnell mimicking Debbie-though unknowingly, fought off fantastic visualizations consisting humanity's varying sorts; folks milling around, having indescribable blasts incommensurably much this once overwhelms one lifetime - within New Loving; conceived during anticipatory periods preceding bare knuckled construction-not alonely whatsoever - despite suggestions by certain idle talks ill-founded portions, how singular drudgeries undertaken by one Ms. little Debbie Charibert - whose parents remained clueless althrough Loving's redevelopment, made Mentone proud by installing elevation unrivalled anywhere else-as concerns peer-counties, Debbie heretofore-commanded many deputies-as is one presently beside co-inspecting - once personal intentions wound up within close knit elementary school associate's circle's understandings.

Master Keighleyworth somehow- eked out enough courage-Debbie admired immediately, young Quinnell usually never spoke much-disrespecting persistent good or bad, Debbie's personal convictions long submitted loquaciousness as unacceptable-albeit little expression or morefolds- thereof carrying much substance, previous Debbie's determinations carried good meanings, illogical utterances sometimes counted, presently, as evening's promenade continued-arms entwined, Quinnell Keighleyworth foolhardily showed courage without earning partner's acquiescence overriding all inhibitive pressures effected by Debbie's proximity, pending pronouncing comments rightly presumed silly, beau's onliest encouragements comprised enviably wide ranging knowledge steeped within 'news about town, or contents occupying county grapevine' -too often observed during exciting moments shrieks sounded involuntarily, or revelries, either- emotions none could attribute New Loving's warrioress hanging tough nearby, but not yet anyhow, indeed, presumptions proved proper –as soon as excited exclamations escaped quivering lips, Debbie's precise reactions consisted mainly surprises,

"Yes, I too agree, even-I, lack capabilities reckoning how I managed pulling this off," little Debbie Charibert informed Quinnell, "look-here, look over everywhere –voilà streets yonder; dwellings, habitations, towering buildings everywhere, far exceeding entire Loving county's five, six, or seven towns currently owns, but I have managed, avenues litter parts, streets-crescents, intersecting roads; one day soon, we ought annex i-80 interstates ferrying visitors en-route diverse parts, or locals back," responses afforded attentive audiences insights, each recognized enviable grips on current affairs –Debbie finished sounding off signature high spirited laughter not customarily eleven year old females', "although master Crispin-" -such designation also being young Quinnell Keighleyworth's other personal aliase, "-on assumptions approvals issue, anyone wanting hangouts should exclaim joyfully, but I scare easily, moreover, Loving's my disposition, our collective psychological states, no?" Quinnell-certainly without further arguments, accepted instructions, agreeing prior hints, warranted reserving commonly accessed exclamations-antecedently giving nicer remarks-way, as one purposeful way– respecting Debbie's admittance moments ago, not 'scare' mistress away. Quick thinking behooved Quinnell onto self-advisement-wherein:- 'never screeching excitedly again however 'electric' moments unveiled', made solitary topics, as– needless empowering another seeking fault one way or another.

First amid serially planned inspections soon ended, New Loving's delighted twosome parted ways once agreements favored later consecutions on today's parting spot-instituting sequels heralding more inspections impacting diverse New Loving parts-today's activities excluded, came forth-after quickly hugging, succeeded by one stolen kiss young Keighleyworth somehow summoned latent cockiness, prior stealing-irregardless if life itself - ended whilst making attempts.

As afore warned, stolen kisses amounted 'scarisome' exploitation Quinnell witnessed elicit frowns multiple levels deep as against pretentiousness-on Debbie's face, such impulsiveness geared toward initiating faint illusion within one's mind–another harbored inhibitions, or equally scary deficiencies thereof, briefly suspecting asininity chosen fellow put up with openly carrying out 'constant companion' duties as fulfilling 'dates' Debbie realized- often helped stave off embarrassing questions touching upon gender impartial associativity, one problem widely detected dogging most elementary school peers seldom observed fraternizing across gender lines, Quinnell's presence provided no such confusing preferences, stolen kiss therefore scared Debbie less.

Daring more impulsive acts –though overwhelmed beyond attempting, Quinnell remained unaware miss Charibert furtively observed departures, somewhat downhearted; one invaluable loyalist-peers generally supposed, not merely during today's inspection, but all through construction's thinnest periods albeit schoolmate's abstentious withholding companionship during recess besides introverted Quinnell Keighleyworth lingering till recess terminated – whether or not conversational points merged–becoming one aesthetically consistent wholesome logic. Earlier on, Miss Charibert's admirers spied male peers flaunting pride-over Quinnell's efforts-pitched as best amongst all sampled, tremendously pleasing alliance's most sedate fellows - who promptly tendered respective '*thing*': concourse spanning alongside proposed i-80 annexed various Loving towns around Mentone, soon afterward, personal architecture installed all over New Loving, resembled county's most well-conceived highway. Quinnell struck as alright, if simply following today's daring kiss stolen without prior permission - establishing sharp-wittedness one could rely on assuming differing circumstances requiring one's services obtained, Keighleyworth men -Debbie learned, owned stands merchandising jumbo hotdog snack never previously enjoyed irrespective after countless envisagement's established certainties only living itself could ever remotely measure against joys New Loving essentially provoked, or satisfaction knowing one holds within during warm nights inside any New Loving's numerous towers - during looming maturity-much such appetite particularly typified one's being –not least per school teacher Peregrine Hildebald's evincements during lessons: how as time passes, bodies communicate subtly, desiring certain nourishment as adult years progresses further, Debbie's heart gladdened, hopefully, Quinnell's many loyalties persists.

Remaining Loving's folks clamorously iterated back whilst good Lego city accommodation lasted, long tacked onto ideas, "methodic madness Phoenix rising's proprietor employed, indeed endured, county officials stood awestruck spectating as each filled necessary applications guaranteeing one desired living spaces, later supplicatorily forwarded papers back requesting Lego City inhabitation allowances soon after inauguration, folks hereinafter, manned excited groups seen milling about unapprehensively proclaiming county-wide tournaments consisting rejoicing folks.

Here Debbie stood holding papers underscoring issue concerning Loving county never boasting beyond one hundred fifty people, maximum two hundred twenty during highest human tides, suddenly confronted forty thousands consisting mostly family'd menfolk's applications essentially pleading Debbie's consideration, each sought viable residential spots fundamentally poised remaining Debbie's evermore living there rather than daydreaming over Loving- or merely wishing on New Loving from across remote lands.

Almost dozing off standing on shorelines sections greeting Beacon Light, effects produced by thumping sounds modern stereo somewhere about emitted, jolted Debbie - as many occupying fantasies whirled around within, prompting fears apropos imminent fates awaiting humankind's second Phoenix-rising, realism dictated transferring underneath Loving County headquarters auspices later on.

Upon squinting, visuals depicted distant executive automobiles approaching along one nearby westerly avenues - as convoy, uncertain visuals connoted approaching intrusions, nevertheless, Judge Trimble's orders stayed effective, no one conceivably reserved permits 'Beacon Light authorities' instituted orders made Trimble, prior verging on any edifice, or -edifices constituting New Loving's surrounding areas habitable by select many Debbie Charibert permitted condominium lodges. Convoys second vehicle recognizably ferried dear Victoria-peers esteemed; 'provider', road paver, guarantor, et-cetera', about. Miss Victoria Van Linden! –Soon, inceptions toward rendezvous warranted revving mottos beneath hoods cars including one accompanying another stylishly decked out carriage whose brand model subsisted one year beyond leading Mercedes, Victoria ferried hither, came alive, propelling automotive masses forward –vehicles every well-meaning local later learned earned general notoriety ferrying working girls around.

Victoria's pulled up first, moments later, Ford's interiors yielded slender tiara clad 'road-paver', accompanying sole Mercedes's occupant pulled up too; accompanying staff; chauffeur Cuthbert Dilsomeworth attended closely by Victoria's personal assistants; Eira Hildegund, Zemislav Littlewood-chauffeuring, but bringing up convoys rear inside entourage's really fancy second carriage chubby Zemislav Littlewood reputed decency - hence Mogul Van Linden issued chauffeuring assignments ferrying family's precious daughter: Victoria Van Linden, hither-thither around town upon employment: constant chauffeuring became onliest repositories-knowledgeable about etymologies –history-perhaps true stories surrounding Lego County everyone riled about ceaselessly, also promising, but mostly pleadingly requesting participation, if society could ever find one promise within ambition's-besides dreams fulfilling reaches -maybe desires too. Gasping, repeatedly, Victoria jumped excitedly --rushing ahead, hugged Debbie. Joy abounded, this constituted many undying dreams all along; expansive landmass parading condominiums, offices, warehouses local factories owned, playgrounds Disney World or also Disneyland-wherever those situated, could emulate. Disentangling affectionate sisterly hug, Victoria-effectuated dance sequels mimicking last occasion –dancing impromptu, till brilliant frolicking moved by pounding music beats resting vehicles provided, overcame Debbie's inhibitions too –soon commenced learning one or two dance steps Victoria instructed through gyrations. Joining hands, another joyous happy dances partly indicating dreams finally reaching realization, broke out, none anymore thought little girl's dependence on ideas older generation passed down, need ever continue after seeing this –great outcomes New Loving's equally influential team surmised, came about due several little girls' unrelenting endeavor Debbie led; Debbie Charibert whom Victoria suddenly learned referencing as 'Mayor Debbie', next time New Loving's financier spoke up, all– as tripping light fantastic continued,

Such agreeable titles as Mayor greatly pleased county's newest high official, however -viewed victoria's affirmations as probatively confirming requirements conferring such permanent title, although– no way-no how-on earth anyone else could act imposingly over Loving mayor's office after single handedly making every resourceful amenity humankind's thriving wanted when inhabiting America's most apt microcosm Loving increasingly became.

Swinging along fine tunes continued still– enthusing two attendant males accompanied by one woman also spectating, heretofore resisting interfering-till two sisters enjoyed respective fills-relishing beautiful New Loving County sprawled nearby, continued waiting. Victoria, quite naturally less enthused, caught grips over avoidable idiosyncrasies upbringing mandated avoiding if possible: acting uncontrollably, halting on going fun event,

"Why?" inquired little Debbie why miss Van Linden unexpectedly ceased gyrating, "explain your hurry-Victoria? -we could loiter bits more amid any event, another half hour admiring working girls realized dreams," -Miss Linden felt terribly pressed, slight dignity remained until mandatory urgency hurriedly leads one inside private commodes, should strike one as precious,

"Not excepting incorrect suspicions, Debbie, let me explain–" -Victoria's explanation compelled attention-being sole financier after all, "mayor's permission hadn't quite issued if boogieing down alongside - meets mayor's official standards, as Mayor, shouldn't one first require permission? –lest my personal interests become distractions,"

"Dearest Victoria, I hadn't thought thusly- come on, let's dance more - if hitting dance floor's all good spirits requires," –as few spectators about saw therefrom, rhythmical gyrations thus continued, until moments-if contemplated, equaled several seconds after harmless Cuthbert Dilsomeworth correctly adjudged new frolicking bouts onsets, increased Mercedes' stereos volumes, instantly flooding more delightful music around surroundings exponentially, causing brief cessation, this time ensuring louder volumes perturbed Mayor immoderately, circumstances warranted enjoyable fun, not intolerably loud volumes interrupting process –this theoretically consisted Debbie's imminent conclusions-

"Why," demanded Debbie, your boggle now comprise?' -as Ms. Van Linden's arm indicated Chauffeur Cuthbert's automobile accompanying hers, facilitating imminent interlocutions Debbie decided listed overridingly as most intriguing explanation no less distracting, versus many more significantly aiding Debbie's subsequent upliftment months succeeding ascension,

"Mercedes beside mine, Debbie, should serve thenceforth on official purposes ferrying New Loving's mayor about,"

"I miss your point, Vicky--" argued Mayor Debbie, "how? -put my county, me particularly, through-" two seconds later, low thunder strikes ruffled atmospheres above, causing quick upward glances,

"Any recollection of your funding's sources?" -began Victoria offering insights regarding mayors 'official carriage': as one symbolizing far beyond an available repurposed automobile provided one county official, often seen lax behind front row seats, such automobiles ferry assigned personnel hither-thither -but also settled ownerships vis-à-vis Loving's first Bentley Arnage- now irredeemably Mayor's permanent doohickey,

"Aha! -finally--!" -mayor's stark surprise prompted several gasps; one quickly following another, though never-mind modernization, county mistress'll soon learn making effective push button implementations, integrated technologies within are plentiful,' thought Debbie --sadly, age fell years short of granting legal permits supporting children beneath eleven behind wheels manipulating carriage's controls, save kindly chauffeur Littlewood allowed dedicated service owed county compel further service,

"Plentiful loyal folks visited here recently: one day or two ago, perhaps three, viewing Beacon Light wonders, soon afterwards- making unanimous love declarations --not merely liking, but loved observances, saying additionally whoever's responsibility ensured erecting countless fixtures within your estate, deserved best favors,"

"Wonderful news-!" mayor found stunning realization-plenty locals still sustained ignorance, identities behind New Loving's most thrilling, remained obscure, "are particularly interested folks discernible? --any knowledge whom?" --followed highly natural question miss Van Linden anticipated hearing Debbie pose, under prevailing circumstances, edifices suddenly rising skywards, till many dominated waterfront's skylines, almost without permission except one inherently accompanying Trimble's orders

"I understand rationale implicit within 'hither': arguments idyllic representations conceivable by great minds, conclusions empowering such purchases --as expensively manufactured bespoke item," interjected Victoria cutting friend's thoughts short,

"Right --your subjective characters think me, Debbie Charibert, Loving's own Mayor?" -inquired proprietress, preceding initial meetings, some hoped ascertained impressions Texan humanity reserved another 'phoenix rising's' proprietor,

"Right," answered Victoria similarly as did Debbie few moments previously, however, this time, Debbie's owned interruptive prerogative,

"Isn't suddenly being mayor noteworthy? –but let's not apply foolish euphemisms yet, Vicky, though we all built New Loving ourselves, our own hands thoroughly dirtied, right?" Loving's proprietress declared proudly, thereafter went on proclaiming little divergent quibbles about diligences costing blood, sweat, also much time, however pointed out free flowing blood during construction's whole affair, never occurred, but certainly suited interfusing into legends later eras observed sprout grapevines repeatedly over time - augmenting Loving's reputation -Victoria again reverted attention, this time, paying former peer now unwittingly accepted as superior, good heed as Mayor's assistants,

"Um-Mayor, we all heaped best efforts onto New Loving, remember? -Did our bests as ordered, contributing all we could; myself, working men, your loyal warrioresses, et-voilà! -Phoenix rising! -reopens, eagerly welcoming guests, visitors - residents alike."

DON M DENN

With joyful edges taken off duo's prancing by sensible arguments, somber moods descended, enough viewing edifices today. Reboarding waiting purpose-built carriages awaiting duties effectuating partings, little Debbie Charibert must return home whereupon encountering more surprises including answering 'all time's' greatest questions any daughter ever faced:– over reacquainting bungalow's safety past lawful childhood curfew imposable by guardians, then, more-concerning sudden unexplained upliftment heralding exalted status compelling school children paying repeated visit in droves bearing flowers, gifts, but most more effigies of family elders, till-given most interesting of grapevines twists, necessity warranted Buchard Charibert-afeard, absconded through rail, temporarily placing daughter underneath far off Sheboygan's keep till certainties broadened regarding family's wellbeing days later.

MAYOR'S INAUGURATION

    *V*iewed as one local daughters retaining imaginations too large wherefore fails fitting Loving County, everyone awarded Debbie much desired approvals permitting unhindered progress, essentially because no one's activities flouted judge's orders-

Dancing far into random night lights, inauguration-minimally narrated - due little else but joy surrounding finally equalizing Loving along peer counties' ranks, reigned throughout–

    '*Such spell binding picture dearest child cast standing atop inauguration podium! –stick - ominously held as soldier would-firearm-fending off dissidents*!' -swore folks departing four-fifths less urgently-as evaluated against lots remaining put, after contained beam meal nourishment Sagard's remittances affected Ticehurst Cholmondeley's supplied - feeding entranced locals, after all, past unattended work fundamentally existed elsewhere around Loving each individual's lives must revisit as everyone carried on, pursuing daily affair effectively putting floods like one Debbie successfully challenged on everyone's behalf, behind.

Hindsight played beneficial roles disclosing countless truths abounding Victoria's past suggestions: on countless many absentee locals requisitioning residential reinstatements New Loving needed even if through statuesque self-effigies every last county person, hewed -truly, right through this opening night, nightly celebrations marginally increased, each event lasting all night long given issues surrounding bettered living accommodations holding center stages.

Mayor's initial public appearances following events engendering Phoenix rising's wake, pended endlessly, but locals endured, hoping providence provided each breviloquent knowledge, such foreknowledge as 'partner identities' on upcoming leader's good list, only fostered hope.

Lego City came alive –active jaywalking Mentone locals resemblant simulacrums-each to every last local, humoresquely milled about indefatigably, dolls' own little vainglorious loud boasting, "*Look everybody, we're Lovingers too! -we– lone state's little people Loving, are*

Lovingers too! -we're part, we're amid thee, we're back!" –one prevalent truth throughout this Mentone night's fiesta–lasting evermore, became -every native's heartfelt dream, one young local, Little Debbie Charibert - fortuitously rendered onto reality through Lego City, through New Loving.

Soon, Mentone's citizenry duly represented each one's self through individual agencies of photo-realistic automatonic mini-humanoid effigies: each substituting every last Mentonian, springing rhythmic steps along jolly beats, Debbie's wondrous music-humanoid effigies heard exclusively - inside this - onliest community even effigies unquestionably entrusted each one's-self once again repopulated Mentone thenceforwards onto many thousands on end, as this enchanting narrative meaningfully touches Debbie Charibert's New Loving where serendipity substantiated 'second phoenix rising', continues each time yet another refreshes memories guarding delightful tales spread over Little Debbie Charibert –Amid great awe, still unconvinced few naysaying malcontents stood stooped low peering closely, observing their own little selves to every last one, living Mentonian dreams inside New Loving. Soon-- amidst hastily approaching, these doom-mongers divested themselves above each one's currently transpiring diversions through each's effigies; dancing, excited conversations, awaiting mayor's reappearance, partying, sightseeing, window shopping too, all progressed simultaneously imbuing minions more liveliness beyond Loving best records contained –revisited Loving county's familiar streets flooded above knee levels thrice - thereat met emptiness --whereupon stumbled upon further failures taking any more steps beyond whence Loving County encountered New Loving.

Time passed, every attempt suddenly subservient floodsters' representing prospecting land grabbers, corrupt politicians, or undesirables exerted, met unanticipated shortfalls, no one-by any means dared challenge ownership nonpareil efforts imbued Miss Charibert, being as holding mayor's sway – amongst many reasons - not least endearing self-affirmed oaths floods never again overwhelmed local parts - not whilst leadership endured.

New Loving's inception loomed, exact moments during any day, afternoon-perhaps dusk or night-as many remarkable oddities continually bustled about, none knew-as Debbie Charibert declined divulging timetables whatsoever no matter whom, still– all duly anticipated mayor Charibert's first appearance. Countless many expected lordly armadas, dignitaries proceeding solemnly, moguls, ostentatiously lionhearted: flaunting higher status quo associations–among other successes, activities integrally connecting looming events-many swore, indicated great excitements come inauguration, disregarding incidental hour transpirations eventuated.

Gung-ho rejoicing over such adorable experiences, numerous witless locals showed emboldened spirits, even pride, charisma about little Debbie - or whichever Mentone's daughters spreading persistently talk indicated, purportedly installed valor besides emotions every local's heart bottled, warrioresses spotted around enclothing uniform top apparels bearing someone's irregular effigies extra strife evidently altered variously on each person's dress. Amok, timidness remained afar due continuing merrymaking experienced by all Loving's constituting seven towns once singularly populated by folks Debbie certainly knew until recently-condemned any unapproved schemes by faceless Loving daughters strenuously attempting re-enacting Mentone's own 'Phoenix rising' incarnation somewhere easy-going folks enjoyed walking or executing unrelated diversions daily.

Dusk one day later heralding first speeches hit town promptly, Lovingers comprised mainly Mentonians but also six surrounding town's natives –swaggered gingerly - given minuscule collective pride affected individuals carry around within, towards Beacon Light en-mass, thereupon chanced upon each person's unique futures --first issued great ululations passably supplanting mounting hysteria, though– solemnly expressed incredulity, as many stared - not possessing faint ideas-visions lying right ahead everyone's perspective, no disciplined persons could engineer such marvelous exploit-but maestros-- mayor's audacity advancing society, staggered many's imaginations.

Soon afterwards, utterly amazed Mentone's diverse humanity witnessed Debbie sashaying alongside Keighleyworth, comparably attired hats; hers: broad brimmed flower-patterned, matching Texan styled cowboys' hat every Texan-Quinnell Keighleyworth befriended must own-if desiring acceptance, produced two balls obscured within coat pocket whence Debbie's earlier activity hurriedly stashed each as events neared, kissed them, soon afterwards returned each back inside Debbie's handbag, Quinnell like Debbie, too- commenced reflecting date's waving actions, hoping not just spectating locals hurled back appreciated nods, but date as well,

"Actions, speak loudly –fables claim," an elderly Mentonian: Mrs. Margaret Littlewood- whose person – surname name: '*Littlewood*' betrayed relativity approximating elderly Margaret, hence possessed sufficient convenience accessing Debbie's bespoke carriage, remarked upon witnessing Debbie's action, others also made agreeing observations thus voiced foregoing self-reminder.

Spoken deliverances persisted atop hastily assembled inauguration platform, but most intriguingly, crowd's attention marveled between; speaker, one brutally portrayed futurism depicting New Loving where installed on Beacon Light's shores, themselves –Standing elevated above any on two juxtaposed adhoc podiums joined together forming one elongated stand, moments after Ticehurst Cholmondeley officially conceded through selfless courtesy, nods, offering unreserved apologies-redressing resentments prosecution's attorney undertakings induced, plus two handshakes, thereby hopefully preventing oaths uttered elsewhere binding too hard, deploy such soothing gratitudes paraphrasing '*thank you*' --Livilda-standing beside teacher Peregrine Hildebald-barrister at law, upon persistently uttering bewilderments, later intimated Debbie,

"Every accused party approaches judgment presumed guilt free–" Ticehurst began-addressing defense team's captain, "greatly appreciated, your side's unequalled travails have saved us all, no longer do naysayers possess arsenals-"

Earth's famous gladiatorial girl proceeded, her remarkable sermons freshly installed within countless memories daily till date, through quidnuncs, grapevines, rumor mills, legends, school lessons –though presently, mirthful– nobody provided reminders like: "–point made, pick up your marbles, run–!":- all around lay ahead of countless vision's, marvel none found fittingly describing words, nor could any wrap minds feeble around as speech progressed,

"Guns inhibit boundaries holding humanities freedoms elsewhere, here, flood--" said mayor continuing address, "but trouble yourselves no more-" -unfortunately, speaker's initial words instituted saddening hushes, such truths as disheartens anyone, as every last one visiting tonight's audience heard-yet continued appraising reactions without pause, "welcome-- my Loving, welcomes all. I am mayor Debbie Charibert" -no one ever made any superlative introductions prior Debbie's ascension, likewise - none afterwards, "I have built this county relying on everyone's goodwill, I shall-as I am presently, continue managing, one day-years ahead, all spent, tired, maybe retired, till your era reaches, disheartens your off-springs shouldering wheels over inheriting Loving - concerning proceeding beyond immediate points our efforts left off, duties abound, duties beckon," one short pause followed whilst glancing around, Debbie standing underneath one spotlight, apparently anticipated accurately ascertaining meanings expressions occupying elder Charibert's face indicated consequent upon divulging wondrous truths during sunset two nights ago-once Sheboygan yielded Mentone both folks, remained powerless pinpointing relative's exact positions amidst throngs, refocused attentions on Loving's humanity unabashedly escaped reality ogling everyone's hometown heroine, but rapt attention as well, as speech continued additionally, "-here's urging all– go about daily concerns as though change's thrived hither all along –our's, here's same old Loving -but cladding new apparels - I say-"

Audiences howled bitter remorse-ridden ululations amid ubiquitous failure discovering Loving's heroine earlier on, others hollered most agonizingly, or loudest each knows how, except harder this time, popular grief excelled previous occasion: 'why providence appointed current flood situations ahead of resolving Loving County's age-old issue?'

Soon after fervid cheering subsided wee-bit enabling folks' refocusing attentions on leader Debbie, each reckoned unoccupied scaffolding signified mayor's entourage's departure following sermon's completion, leaving Livilda, Zoe, Victoria-besides several alliance workmen's furthering sworn duties upon each becoming instrumental erecting New Loving, tonight-- earned new duties overseeing remaining inauguration activities.

Some brief tete-à-tete kept-two foremost warrioresses occupied,

"My! –I see standing alongside some other fellow, famed working girls' faceless benefactor audiences observed arriving earlier on flanked by event's smallest possible complimenting security detail? Inauguration, Debbie ascertained later, bore unreserved-but healthy social changes Sagard Summers-known characteristically as 'events avoider' always wanted –not least tonight's selfless bequests philanthropic Sagard Summers corporation promoted alongside satisfied beneficiaries –this being Aubourc's multiloquency - perhaps duty ensured, created awareness through published statistics listing charity's recipients, due ensuant disclosures, compulsory attendance by unconnected local peers seeking furtively handed largesse too increased marginally. Sagard Summers stood thereabouts several cars away signaling Debbie-exiting inauguration arena, pensive over many difficult roads Loving traveled until Mayor Debbie. No feelings surpassed standing firm beside one- championing causes everyone forsook,

"Ah! -Voilà-famed warrioress Charibert! -Amazing!"

Giving away smart devices proved somewhat-one error Summers blamed deep personal financial cuts on, but one surprisingly observed all over as arousing much rejoicing, free donations paid off, allowing ill-gotten fortunes-many never ceased supposing, generate good,

"My-oh-my!" exclaimed Debbie espying indicated gentleman: tall Sagard Summers peripherally, whilst continuing away alongside warrioresses-anyhow - once Victoria finished introductions between strangers whose unwavering support besides patronage ensured fairings benevolently donated-all involved agreed, wound up enabling constant communications everyone knew saw everyone through, as Admiral Sagard Summer's mimicry omitted choreography: no prior practical sequence existed - tonight's; orchestrators, visitors, et cetera, must first honor learning prior appearing synchronous observing hitherto agreed upon actions, or remain dignified around tonight's coinciding public,

"Everyone–" announced Debbie additionally whence she'd halted by others aware microphones pinned on to apparels still transmitted amplified sound --as though information about divulged hadn't sounded out of another seconds–ticking up one minute, "stands our- 'premier alliance man'!"

Sagard Summers settling many internal biases privately, evinced nothing could ever bring about surrendering wits become however much eagerness prompts, nor unabashedly give chase either. Waving still- stood by watching as Loving' young female entourage disappeared, enveloped by surrounding's nearest umbra. Short whiles passing saw Sagard watch surrounding darkness rob many viewers evening's most desired object,

"Impressive--" muttered Admiral Sagard assured tonight's companion apprehended underlying meanings,

"As will I, if ever either of us are later indulged any acknowledgments," companion Ferry warned master Summers,

"I long meeting soon–"

"As do I."

"Mayor has our undying support-"

"As-our's --but for your unending patronage-dear," Admiral immediate business ogling potentials prevented espying an elitist lady's approach – which terminated shortly following retreat elsewhere soon after realizing Sagard Summers' own very personality monopolized attentions in immediate vicinities being as very young girls clamored about seeking autographs --moments later approached whereupon, someone's voice hitherto unaccompanying perceived associates about, cut through Debbie's ebbing consciousness - addressing certain issues regarding patronage, but also support- jolting mayoral attentions onto just arrived well clad middle aged citizen beaming joyfully, apparently peculiarly high society's: though none certainly guesses correctly; whether of --darkness's, or of --daylight's: Aubourc beautified onto altered perceptions appropriately much younger womanhood's - by two decades perhaps three, confounded Debbie. Briefly deciphering if any special significances inherently juxtaposed unfamiliar person's 'support' alongside 'patronage' within same expression, till-- aha!---realization-! --Aubourc! -stopping by hadn't cost any extra efforts, obviously, Shadowbrook's clerk loved visiting inaugurations, tonight, hopefully seeking exploitable privileges personally congratulating Loving's mayor.

"My goodness!" -gasped Debbie transfixed, scarcely knowing any more appropriate words conveying surprises appellatively identifying almost strange woman by name correctly– "Mrs.– Mrs.–!" -another gasp– recollections correspondingly reminded lady-not excepting occasion's celebrity - transpirations during encounters one fateful night general store received no other customers, encouraged two lingering smiles, "am I glad we meet again–elder working girl, couldn't really be you Aubourc, aren't you?"

"Aubourc-dear, saying– mayor's successfully reached far extents less fantastic men failed, Aubourc'll do just fine, Debbie," -Aubourc intending keeping conversation alive-preveniently addressed mayor some more, "I'm afraid your imagination wasn't off --marvelous!"

"Much obliged Aubourc, those words mean very much, all working girls appreciate."

Somewhat strangely abstracted-perhaps by surrounding events, or overawed by tonight's inspirational visuals Debbie's person amounted, Aubourc's response edged matters nearer queer ends,

"Summarily dear, one rose stalks amidst one dozen, does wither unto waste, while one; one represents every girl involved, young or old, reaches fruition --Debbie, I too, go by 'working girl'," Aubourc informed county mayor words spoken during initial meetings that evening,

"I dare say, I do dare say--" Aubourc retorted solemnly replying mayor's information-urgent occupation elsewhere mandated considerations over fleeting time; indeed, departures inflexibly beckoned, but Aubourc refused Debbie's alibies supporting abrupt departures, citing-- important new information forwarded by equipment's donors, as well as two scribble written notes ordered secured by Mentone's benevolent Admiral - requesting personal meetings, county office must retrieve alongside other items county's main general store since-supplying all warrioresses' other useful effects holds waiting – forthwith. Young Mayor's decision postponing egressions another ten minutes-hearing Aubourc out, seemed proper, here stood proudly, an honorable lady: without whose timely intervention, lately events potentially jested efforts onto humility whereas four sultry single dollars encouraging budding sister's aspirations over two afore-utilized smart phones costing five times more apiece, could not have rescued them. On this day, Aubourc learned then unapparent truths about identities ninety-five blustery nights ago two young unassuming young Mentone girls emerged out of Mentone darkness.

Happy reunions do end eventually, therewithal ended inauguration day's, when enchanted women parted ways promising another reconvening on appointed dates thence recoup all donated odds besides ends.

All around, great quibbles accompanying continuing discussions interpreting many anticlimaxes little known girls club: warrioresses, hammered upon land grabber's dreams finally setting many individual ambitions further into oblivion, reached heavenly heights,

"Cheers all, much appreciated," Debbie muttered underneath bathed breathes somewhat assured locals scattered jubilantly all around heard mayor's heartfelt salutations, however, obliging Aubourc, dearest Aubourc, Sagard Summers too, "I Debbie, Mayor-Charibert-actually, believe those could bring Loving's future great good –but first, I mayor--" –as Debbie put matters, "--must possess confidence towards any such persons," then whispering mostly, added, "not necessarily Ticehurst or several alike-" -indeed, involving such needlessly could worsen matters all desire resolved, thereafter, mayor knew, smooth sailing inclinations awaits county.

Sauntering off toward Beacon Light's furthest parts-or nearing thereabouts through space inch after inch incrementally, mayor embraced brief solicitude - intending disabusing Quinnell some closeness, if only momentarily.

Picking up one solitary stone Beacon light's gently ebbing waters regurgitated on sandy grounds, mayor's tensed muscles enabled airborne propulsion fromward directions already traversed, thereafter raced, intending retrievals. Similarly performed Quinnell Keighleyworth, oblivious partner-initially craving solitude, now intended sudden halts-- causing boy's front ends colliding forcefully against girl's behinds-nearly upsetting evening's affairs had Debbie toppled. Regaining balance, Quinnell's inquiry as respects already derived feelings should one suddenly ram another's backsides; much like guilty actions freshly seared into partners' memories,

"Ha-ha," laughed little Debbie, "not funny,"

"Alright, pardon me," -Quinnell's apology might have issued late, until partner acceded, self-advisement favored refusing any more foolish errors attributingly bellicose-if peculiar understandings dignified just executed maneuvers correctly, Quinnell, preteen generation's free-swinging individual, similarly set personal inauguration day's activities-motionward not hoping Debbie caused misery –no, not so, Quinnell simply hoped companionship tonight providing pleasant surprises –not after untold exertions rebuilding Loving.

"Debbie," recommenced beau twelve seconds later - picking up petered out chitchat, once again faced directions going afar beyond every other one's immediate reach –as far behind, Loving's admiration continued, "I thought briefly about talks involving us later on,"

"No, Quinnell, topic centered on diverse matters not on your person, Vicky- Debbie's fond reference given New Loving's official Deputy, wouldn't needlessly waste breaths on anyone placed lower, we touched minds on how one always subsists one decision abreast total life's alterations, if slightly more strife apply."

Continuity cued Debbie's remarks save Quinnell's interruption following genuine confusion,

"I'm rather disappointed, my understandings fall short of your explanations," folks spoke truths sometimes, this unabashedly sincere admission however impressed Quinnell's; as response, following ruminations over instructions fourteen hours previously during moments engaging Mrs.

Charibert on talks over school's constant crush quite regularly talked about-as– often providing assistance tackling matters Bessie Haynes schooling provisioned pupils.

Doubtful over any suitable subsequent actions, poked hardest musterable jab Quinnell's navel least anticipated --taking countless retaliations whose justification incrementally warrants shrugging off all as time passes-ever tightening friendship onto maturity together, assuming only if Quinnell prevails over competing 'suitor's list –proved sole instigating impetus inspiriting recompense fitting jolting Debbie almost

Using sufficient vigor, Debbie's extended index finger harpooned forward, intending probing percolatively through poor Mr. Keighleyworth's omphalic hollow umbilical cords once occupied. Agonizing unmanageably, stricken lad doubled up, falling prostrate face first on Beacon Light's sandy earth-proximately close by Debbie's feet firmly planted apart - terribly sore, thereby executing era's most embarrassing face plant atop terra firma well within New Loving's territories, whilst clutched abdomen parts throbbed painfully, making howling continue as moments added upwards till few minutes elapsed, Debbie realize afore-described finger probing activity appreciably discomforted Quinnell --Debbie basically followed Ayleth's wisdom, unsure if any sensible interpretations partner's show authenticates, if not child's play - exists. –Or maybe cue Quinnell partner's endless expectations afterward! -alright! - alright! -No worries! -never mind, maybe taking all available help later on into account, Quinnell deserved one more finger poke– " B u m p i n g another's behind unexpectedly without permission painfully reminds one - assault still carries on, Quinnell assuredly reckons now? --don't you Quinnell-?" Mayor Debbie required disclosures, as dainty legs once again gratified belle with increasing distance beau needed covered once spinning around completed, Debbie continued, retreating farther whereat grownup years cordoned any further intrusions acquaintances often posed --continually riling compatriots could never catch up –still enthusing:-- how one young local defied all odds–resettling all's mini selves comfortably inside another 'Phoenix rising', to gradually progress towards many tomorrows this day, as each anticipated retiring home after one day's activities well spent gloriously restarting Loving, locals regarded deepening dusk briefly, soon thereafter, headed home towards rekindling lifestyles previous disguises guaranteed each.

On this night, Little Debbie Charibert moved further away onto life's prime - embracing regions whence far more life's frills fashioning once Mentone heroine city's prominent physician, reached inhabitants –permanently beyond hometown folks forever admiring New Loving abdicated then --enchanted beyond belief by living breaths once little Debbie breathed into Loving --always enjoining Quinnell Keighleyworth-stunned beyond comprehending any inhibitions over more painful signals, yet, constantly pursued– as partnership persisted always afterwards.

End

BLURB

Soon after deciding—there seems no common grounds changing feelings amongst diverse generations—by Loving county's younger folks – regarding state of affairs—following environmentally unfriendly and cataclysmal floods, by leader of the younger pack—Little Debbie Charibert, she unceremoniously secures efforts onto helms of momentarily abandoned affairs of Loving County of Texas – where continuous bustle of living—until recently – never really comprised normal sound—in orientating Loving towards her desired trajectory.

None being more gratified with
steam rolling faceless tycoons pursuing gruesome intentions to rob local Loving county folks of its status of quaint little town all knew her to be – with vanquishing swift kicks in their guts, than one unassuming young local about to be deprived possession of thoroughgoing memories of Loving County, inquired of collaborating associates; what it was that ails them wildly upon—perceiving land developers suddenly incapable of governing their usurpatory greed to supervene farmlands where ought be city blocks there at home?

Thus— dwelling quietly on their own pleasant solitude and bad dispositions, playmates—just as passionate in beliefs, encounter men at work guarded by muscle clad bulldozers—to begin halting work before corn stalks grow in lieu of sand castles / homes—

Gearing for confrontation against workmen—Loving county's young marauders conjectured were cut from the same bolt of shabby—as the rest of older generation – and hadn't exactly brought a load of joy, eagerly cast workmen as cynical outsiders – for being honest with opinions of staying many yards shy of dangerous bulldozers, else—

Wondering what purpose laxity would serve Loving to catch its demise they way it hustled for it by hosting flood, dared to defy great odds with relentless work—hour after hour, day after day – till phoenix rising emerged from legends ro be true in Loving. Nobody had ever seen a thing like it before – as tower after tower, homestead after habitable homestead—hewed out of Loving's own sands, might's of resourceful loyal stalwarts, and Little Debbie Charibert's insight – suddenly stood prominent all over Loving's waterfront.

Standing aside to assess reactions by folks she knows are truly treacherous, but can't quite say what they think of her now—inspecting New Loving—she single handedly erected, this enterprising young girl invites kinsfolks once impressioning her—only adults know the way forward – to move right into welcoming homes of choice – in the new Loving County —and for many eons thereafter – Loving—in the minds of all – held firm amongst any other county.

Printed in the USA
CPSIA information can be obtained
at www.ICGtesting.com
LVHW041225110624
782902LV00001B/176